Interviews with the Damned
Documents on the Determination of
Soul Interment and Punishment

M. Maker

I must say thank you to my wonderful wife. I could not have written and gotten this book together without her, her knowledge, and her support.

What are people saying about Hell Exposed

"No Comment" God.

"Someone is Going to Pay" Satan.

"All lies, it is all lies" Belial, Lord of Lies.

"Hell is clean, safe and a sanitary place."
Beelzebub, Lord of Flies.

"I feel the demons are too soft on the damned
souls." Vlad Dracul, The Impaler.

"The Demon games are cruel and unnecessary." Soul
condemned to be sports equipment.

"Send more politicians, bring back the Reign of
Terror and the Guillotine!" Ted, Demon
Interviewer.

Prologue

Through several rituals, rites, briberies, liaisons, lunches, strip-club meetings, and one stormy night at the crossroads with an almost live chicken, we have acquired these documents for you to see the truth.

These documents were obtained through the diligence of a dissatisfied mid-level bureaucrat on the inside of Hell. They risked nothing to bring them to us.

Here are twenty true documents to expose Hell and its mistreatment of damned souls. These documents expose Hell for what it is: a place where demons abuse their power. These demons enjoy abusing these lost souls and these are the documents proving it. There is almost a dedication to mistreatment of the lost souls. Some of the descriptions are vivid, cruel, and just not very nice. We have not altered these documents in any way after receipt from the mid-level bureaucrat.

These documents are on the determination of damnation status interviews. We have to assume that certain information is gathered from these interviews to help the bureaucracy run Hell; but we are not sure what kind of information if it is even important.

DOCUMENT 1

INTERVIEW: 189009I7S

Interview: I8900917s

Demon: Tom-989865691–86I96634*e4

Soul

Given Name: Jason John Prince

Also Known as: Royal Jay Jay

Occupation: Burglar/Thief

Transcribed by: Demon Transcriber #0907987876765-3457a3b

Transcript

Tom-989865691-86I96634*e4 (From here on referred to as "Tom".): It is my job to interview you to determine your damnation status and/or clarification of specifics of your level of damnation in hell.

Jason John Prince (From here on referred to as "Mr. Prince".): {unintelligible mumbles…with a squeak or whistle}

Mr. Prince: Man, I am Royal Jay Jay, the coolest thief this side of East 72nd Street.

Tom: Your given name please.

Mr. Prince: Fuck you, that is the only name you are going get out of me.

Tom: Okay, you need some instruction.

(Tom reached out and removed Mr. Prince's left eye and the left side of the face. He also used his prehensile tail to enter Mr. Prince from behind approximately two inches above his anus and split Mr. Prince into two equal pieces)

(Interviewed paused while Mr. Prince's soul re-constitutes to human body form.)

Tom: Please state your given name.

Mr. Prince: Jason John Prince.

Tom: It is my job to interview you to determine your damnation status and/or clarification of specifics of your level of damnation in Hell. Do you understand what I am saying to you?

Mr. Prince: Ah, yeah sure I hear what you are saying.

Tom: Mr. Prince, do you know what that means?

Mr. Prince: Yeah, that dude Sharen explained it to me. I died and now I am in Hell. I asked him how long, he just said, "What does time matter in Hell".

Tom: You mean, Charon, and he is correct you are dead, and time does not really matter in Hell. All that matters in Hell is the damnation, which brings us back to your own damnation, and this interview to determine some facts of your death.

Mr. Prince: Damnation, you mean like going to Hell damnation? Wait, I can change, I don't want to go to hell.

(Mr. Prince started softly sobbing.)

Tom: First, you do NOT have to worry about if you are going hell; you are already here. We are just trying to determine the correct torture for your punishment.

(Mr. Prince broke into crying and sobbing at this moment, the interview stopped for two years one month and thirteen days while Mr. Prince sobbed in a cell)

(Continuation of Interview)

Tom: Mr. Prince we are now going to continue your interview. We, as an administration, are striving to improve our damnation determination process. We have some specific questions about the night that you passed from mortality. Now will you please state your name, for the continuation process.

Mr. Prince: I remember you…. you… you, you ripped me apart.

(Mr. Prince began to cry softly gain)

Tom: Yes, I am, please do not make me delay the interview. I have some simple questions that you should be able to answer.

Mr. Prince: I will answer what I can, just please don't put me back in the cell.

Tom: On the day of your death, you had decided to burgle someone, is that correct?

Mr. Prince: Yep, I needed a score.

Tom: How did you select your victim?

Mr. Prince: Well, see how it was I was at this gun show, looking for a pigeon.

Tom: Can you explain "pigeon"?

Mr. Prince: You know a pushover, a cash cow.

Tom: You mean an easy victim.

Mr. Prince: Yeah, but the gun show was full of people with guns, I mean everyone had a gun, there were guns everywhere, hell the little old lady pigeons were buying guns.

Tom: How did you select your "pigeon"?

Mr. Prince: Yeah that was easy, see as I walked around scoping out the pigeons, I found a table with no guns on it, no nothing to do with guns. But man was he making money, he was making hundreds every time...

Tom: So, what was on this table?

Mr. Prince: Knives, I mean big knives, little knives, swords, axes… but not one gun and people were buying them. I guess he made them or something.

Tom: He was a bladesmith?

Mr. Prince: No! He made knives!!

(At this time Tom's prehensile tail had went behind Mr. Prince, and assumed the striking position but did not strike)

Tom: Mr. Prince, a bladesmith makes knives, that is what the profession is called.

Mr. Prince: Yeah, he made knives.

Tom: You selected this bladesmith to rob, what did you do after you made the decision?

Mr. Prince: So, I hung out in the parking lot until it closed, and was gonna follow him to his hotel, but you know what he lived near, he went home. What a score! I don't only get his money and his knives. I was gonna hit his house too, and you know what, he had a workshop, I knew some of those tools were gonna pay big time… oh man what a pigeon.

Tom: You followed him to his place of residence, where he has a workshop. What did you do then?

Mr. Prince: I was gonna wait until he went to sleep, no luck there. He went to that nice workshop, turned on some kind of heater. Why would he do that, it's hot as hell …wait…well not that hot…

Tom: I understand what you mean. He turned on a "heater," please continue after that.

Document I Interview: I8900917s

Mr. Prince: Yeah, so he turned on this heater, put on this apron like he was gonna cook or something. Then he took a long stick with a short thick stick on the end and put it in the heater. I guess that is how he makes those knives. Talk about an easy pigeon, he put on some dark glasses, and then could you believe it; he put on loud music… hell, I didn't even have to sneak up on him….

Tom: Just so I understand, the "pigeon" put on dark glasses, and loud music, while he worked?

Mr. Prince: Yeah man it was easy…I had a knife…but I saw one of those big knives he makes on the way in so I grabbed it, man it looked sharp,…it was like one of those machetes from that movie…with the guy with all the …machetes….I don't know the name but it was like that…and it looked sharp.

Tom: I believe you mean the movie "Machete" with Danny Trejo.

Mr. Prince: Yeah, that bad mother, so I walked up on this guy just like Machete. I looked like a bad MF, I had a machete, I was looking tough.

Tom: As I understand it, you grabbed the machete, and approached the chosen victim.

Mr. Prince: Yeah, man, I had him, I mean he was just pulling that long stick out of that heater, I walked up to him…what did I say, oh yeah, "Time to die, Pendejo."

Tom: What do you remember after you spoke to the victim?

Mr. Prince: That's odd, all I remember is the smell of burning pork…

Afternote: It has been determined that Mr. Prince approached his intended victim while the said victim was working with his forge. The Victim had a red-hot glowing knife shaped object, on the end of a long stick, the stick and object could be considered a spear that was glowing hot. The bladesmith used it as a spear and impaled Mr. Prince through the heart.

Damnation Recommendation:

Initial recommendation is the soul be interned to the Demon Forge area with a Nickelback/Justin Bieber audio feedback loop while strapped under a demon forge, with damnation review in seven-hundred-fifty years.

DOCUMENT 2

INTERVIEW: 189999T6S-A

Interview: I89999t6s-a

Demon: Ted-98986569I-8765309*e4

Soul

Given Name: Theodore Roosevelt Pollard

Also Known as: Teddy

Occupation: Bank Robber/petty thief

Transcribed by: Demon Transcriber #0907987876765-3457a3b

Transcript

Ted 98986569I-8765309*e4 (From here on referred to as "Ted".): It is my job to interview you to determine your damnation status and/or clarification of specifics of your level of damnation in hell.

Theodore Roosevelt Pollard (From here on referred to as "Mr. Pollard".): Say what Asshole? Who the fuck are you to judge me?

(Ted proceeds to reach across the table and inserts his hand into Mr. Pollard's mouth and twists the jaw, removing it from the damned soul. Ted then puts the jaw on the table)

Ted: I am Ted 98986569I-8765309*e4, the demon that is assigned to determine where in Hell you are supposed to go for your damnation. I am not the one who gets to judge you, I am just a bureaucrat who is assigned to deal with your damnation in Hell. Do you understand?

Mr. Pollard: (mumbles something but it is unintelligible)

(Mr. Pollard nods his head up and down while making the sounds)

Ted: Mr. Pollard I will take that as an affirmative, please reach down, pick up your jaw, and replace it on your face, it will attach at least enough for you to communicate during this interview.

(Mr. Pollard reaches down, picks up the jaw and places it on his face. Ted heals him slightly)

Ted: Can you speak?

Mr. Pollard: Yeah…

(Ted, lifts his hand)

Mr. Pollard: Yes Sir, yes sir I can speak.

Ted: Good, now what is your full given name?

Mr. Pollard: Teddy.

Ted: I said your full given name.

Mr. Pollard: Theodore Roosevelt Pollard, my mom like Theodore Roosevelt.

Ted: We know; she is in the Theodore Roosevelt Rape Room.

Mr. Pollard: What, what do you mean she is in a rape room?

Ted: Yes, she allowed sexual assaults of children in her care, including you. It seemed like a fitting damnation.

Mr. Pollard: She was a sixty-six-year old, what kind of bastards are you, she was a 66-year-old woman...

Ted: Mr. Pollard what part of Demons, in Hell do you not understand?

(Mr. Pollard attempts to jump over the table to assault Ted at this time, Ted caught him with his hand and held him)

Mr. Pollard: You fucking bastards, you fucking bastards, you fucking bastards.

Ted: Mr. Pollard, point of fact, you are the bastard, and the one fucking the bastards was, in fact, your mother, on several occasions, sometimes with several. That is in fact how you were conceived.

(Mr. Pollard begins sobbing while Ted holds him over the table with one hand)

Mr. Pollard: Why would you tell me something like that, I mean my mother in a rape room, and that I was conceived in a threesome. I mean what the fuck?

Ted: Mr. Pollard I did not say threesome, I believe you call it a "train". The reason I told you is we get so few perks in this job, that is one of the ones I enjoy.

(Ted drops Mr. Pollard into his chair and conjures leather straps around Mr. Pollard's arms and legs. Mr. Pollard continues to sob lightly)

Ted: Now that I have had a little fun, we must continue with the interview. The records show you died during a bank robbery. We have a few questions about your actions during the robbery and your selection of your victim.

Mr. Pollard: Fuck you, I'm not gonna say a fucking word.

Ted: Mr. Pollard, I really do not have time for you to be difficult. I will explain it to you in a way you will understand.

(Ted moves the table to the side, reaches down, violently removes Mr. Pollard's genitals, and proceeds to shove them into Mr. Pollard's mouth down his throat. Mr. Pollard has no choice but to swallow. Ted then heals Mr. Pollard's genitals. Ted repeats this action three more times, then replaces the table in front of Mr. Pollard.)

Ted: Mr. Pollard will you now cooperate?

Mr. Pollard: Yes, god yes, I will, I will answer any questions you have, I will tell you everything…please don't do that again.

Ted: We are familiar with the bank robbery, you and Thomas Nathan Thomas, I believe you know him as "Tommy" decided to rob the bank on the first of the month. We know this was decided because you wanted the checks the senior citizens get on the first. We have some questions about after you entered the building.

Mr. Pollard: Yeah…that is right how did you know that…nobody was around when we were talking about it.

Ted: Demons, Hell, the book of your life. We know a lot.

Mr. Pollard: Oh, ok what do you want to know?

Ted: You selected a couple to take hostage. We would like to know more about why you selected the couple and what happened when you did.

Mr. Pollard: Oh yeah, the old couple with the guy in the wheelchair. Seemed pretty obvious, I mean they were old as shit, and the guy was crippled.

Ted: Please tell me anything you noticed about the guy in the wheelchair.

Mr. Pollard: He was old, he was crippled in a wheelchair, that's about it. Oh yeah, he had a hat on…it said, "Omaha Beach". I remember thinking I have never heard of that beach around here.

Ted: Mr. Pollard, that beach is not located near where you died; it is located in Normandy, France. Did you notice anything else?

Mr. Pollard: Not really …I grabbed him, jerked him out of his wheelchair. Wait he had a pin on his collar that stabbed my hand, that is when I punched him. Gotta, say for an old fuck he sure can take a punch.

Ted: Did you notice what the pin was, or what it said?

Mr. Pollard: No…did not really notice…wait I remember it said "UDT." I mean whadda fuck does that mean "UDT"

Ted: Do you remember anythi*ng else?

Mr. Pollard: Not really, wait yeah, I remember a foot, a foot hit me in the face. Wait, the fucker kicked me. How the fuck did he kick me; he was crippled. That's not fucking fair I mean, a crippled kicked me.

(Ted conjured a ball gag on to Mr. Pollard silencing him at this time)

Ted: Mr. Pollard for your information, Omaha Beach is part of the beach where the Allied forces attacked Germany on D-day. UDT stands for underwater demolition team, the teams that were required to swim underwater and destroy obstacles in the way of the invasion. Your victim was on Omaha Beach, and was a member of the UDT units. To put it in terms you will understand, he was a REAL BADASS. Last, your victim did not kick you in the face. He removed his prosthetic leg and beat you to death with it.

Document 2 Interview: I89999t6s-a

Afternote:

Mr. Pollard's lack of knowledge of basic history led him to select a victim that was not used to being a victim. He assumed someone old and in a wheelchair was helpless.

Damnation Recommendation:

Mr. Pollard should be interned in the Acheron River of Pain on a beach barricade known as a hedgehog, with a video connection of his mother's damnation fed to him alternating with Barney videos switching every hour, with a damnation review in two-hundred-twenty-five years.

Damnation adjustment:

It was determined that having the soul watch an alternating view of his mother's damnation and Barney videos was deemed too cruel. The Barney videos have been removed.

Interview: I89999t6s-b

Demon: Ted-989865691-8765309*e4

<u>Soul</u>

Given Name: Thomas Nathan Thomas

Also Known as: Tommy

Occupation: Bank Robber/Petty Thief/Child Abuser

Transcribed by: Demon Transcriber #09079878767653457a3b

Transcript

Ted-989865691-8765309*e4 (From here on referred to as "Ted".): It is my job to interview you to determine your damnation status and/or clarification of specifics of your level of damnation in hell. I am already familiar with your partner Theodore Roosevelt Pollard which you know as "Teddy".

Thomas Nathan Thomas (From here on referred to as "Mr. Thomas".): I don't know what the fuck you are talking about, I am innocent.

Ted: You seem to need some motivation, I do not believe you understand where you are, and the current situation that you are in.

(Ted conjures leather straps on Mr. Thomas' body restraining him to the chair, complete with gag to silence him. Large scarab beetles begin to crawl up from the floor and begin feasting on Mr.

Thomas. Ted has pulled out "War and Peace" by Leo Tolstoy and begins reading.)

Interview Stopped

(While Mr. Thomas body is eaten by the Scarab beetles, regenerates and is re-eaten, Ted proceeds to read War and Peace by Tolstoy, The Hobbit and The Lord of the Rings trilogy by Tolkien, The Death Gate Cycle series by Margaret Weis and Tracy Hickman, the complete works of Terry Pratchett twice, The Wheel Of Time by Robert Jordan and the Odyssey by Homer.)

Interview Continued

(Ted conjures the Scarab Beetles away.)

Ted: Mr. Thomas do you wish to adjust your statement of innocence, and your wish to give a "fuck".

Mr. Thomas: Unintelligible grunting noises through the ball gag.

Ted: I will take that as a yes.

(Ted conjures the ball gag away. Mr. Thomas begins to sob)

Ted: Mr. Thomas, please state your full name.

Mr. Thomas: They call me T. N.T., 'cause I am dynamite.

(A scarab beetle appears on the table. Mr. Thomas starts struggling to get away.)

Ted: Mr. Thomas no one, but you, calls you T.N.T., would you like to adjust your statement?

(Scarab beetle crawls slowly towards Mr. Thomas, tears are now rolling down Mr. Thomas' face)

Mr. Thomas: Okay, Okay, oh god okay, goddamn anything, just get that thing away from me.

Ted: Mr. Thomas please state your full given name.

Mr. Thomas: Thomas Nathan Thomas, goddamn it's Thomas Nathan Thomas.

Ted: Mr. Thomas I am here to clarify some specifics so we can punish you correctly, we do not want non-efficient damnation. Your answers will help us determine type and length of damnation. Do you understand?

Mr. Thomas: I guess.

Ted: Mr. Thomas, your answers will determine the hell you will endure.

Mr. Thomas: Hell? You mean like hellfire and brimstone? Burning, demons with pitchforks…burning my soul.

(Ted becomes a six-foot-six muscular red tinted scowling classic pitchfork welding demon with curved horns, then returns to the classic middleman pen welding business suit look with prehensile tail.)

Ted: There is no need to stereotype demons; we do not ALL actually get the pleasure of burning your soul, some of us are stuck in this bureaucracy, and do not get to do the burning.

(Mr. Thomas is now quiet, calm, and trying to go into shock, which is impossible for a soul in Hell. His eyes locked on the scarab beetle, which is taking very small steps toward him.)

Mr. Thomas: I am in Hell? Damn I wasn't that bad.

Ted: Yes, you were, you were a bad petty thief, you attempted to rob a bank, but what really damned your soul is your abuse of children, you hit them, and burned them. Child abusers automatically go to Hell, we like getting child abusers down here, it is some of our best torture entertainment.

Mr. Thomas: (whispers) Oh.

Ted: The questions we have are pertains the day you died.

Mr. Thomas: I died.

Ted: Yes, Mr. Thomas you are dead and in Hell, now do I need to feed the scarab beetles or are you ready to proceed.

Mr. Thomas: I am ready to proceed. Please, no more beetles.

Ted: On the day you died, you and your partner, a Theodore Roosevelt Pollard, which you know as Teddy, attempted to rob a bank. You had selected to rob the bank so you could steal the money from senior citizens. Is this correct?

Mr. Thomas: Yeah, we were gonna score big.

Ted: We know you went in, grabbed two hostages. Your partner grabbed an old soldier, while you grabbed the soldier's wife.

Mr. Thomas: Yeah, the old man was in a wheelchair, and that old biddy was walking but she had two large purses, I mean how much money do you have to have to carry two purses.

Ted: Just for clarification, she was not carrying two purses, she was carrying a knitting bag and a purse.

Mr. Thomas: How the hell was I to know that?

(The scarab beetle started moving towards Mr. Thomas, and a second one appears beside of the first one)

Ted: I will point out that these beetles have a taste for rudeness. As I understand they love it, it is a quirk of Hell.

Mr. Thomas: What the fuck does that mean?

(The two scarab beetles go directly towards Mr. Thomas. Several hundred scarab beetles appear on the floor around Mr. Thomas' feet, Mr. Thomas starts screaming. Ted pulls out a personal recording device and turns it on. During the next hour Mr. Thomas is screaming, Ted is bobbing his head in time with the screams, similar to what a human would do for music. Mr. Thomas finally stops screaming. Ted turns off the recording device and puts it in his pocket.)

Ted: Thank you for the screams, nothing goes better in our music than the screams of a child abuser. But now we must continue with the interview.

Mr. Thomas: My screams are music to you?

Ted: Yes, what did you expect demons to enjoy?

Mr. Thomas: (unintelligible mumbles) This really is Hell?

Ted: Back to your hostage, can you tell me about what happened.

Mr. Thomas: Yeah, I mean Yes Sir, I grabbed the old biddy.

(Scarab began twitching.)

Mr. Thomas: I mean the elderly lady.

(Scarab stopped moving.)

Mr. Thomas: Yes, the elderly lady, I grabbed one of her purses, and opened it up. I was gonna grab her money but all I saw was thread, I mean it was full of thread and one large, I guess you would call it a needle.

Ted: Yes, that would be a knitting needle, one of a pair.

Mr. Thomas: Oh yeah, that Bi… I mean elderly lady stabbed me with the other one, right in the Nu…, I mean between my legs.

Ted: Correct, she did stab you. What else do you remember?

Mr. Thomas: I turned towards Teddy as he went down and I saw, wait did I see the old ba… I mean the elderly gentleman, beat Teddy with a leg?

Ted: You are correct your associate was beaten to death with a prosthetic leg.

Mr. Thomas: Wow, what a way to go, I mean Wow.

Ted: We need to continue with your questions. What happened then?

Mr. Thomas: I had a needle stuck in my nu...groin area. It was painful, so I turned and saw Teddy getting beat to death with a leg. I bent over, I felt a pressure, wait in my ass? Yeah, I felt something pushing in my ass. Then I hear a bang, and pain, all I can think that happened is one of the security guards shot me. Well at least I didn't get beat to death by an old man with his leg, -what could be more embarrassing?

Ted: You are correct Mr. Thomas, you did not get beat to death by an old man, but I am not sure you would consider the truth better than getting beat to death by a plastic leg?

Mr. Thomas: Wait, what do you mean?

Ted: To put it in terms you might understand. After the old "biddy" stabbed you in the dick, and yes, she hit your dick, which is impressive for how small it is. You bent over in pain, turning away from her, towards her husband. When you did, she reached in her purse and pulled out a four inch, three-fifty-seven magnum revolver, and in her haste and excitement to point it at you she penetrated your anus with the barrel. To be very accurate, she shoved it up your ass and pulled the trigger…twice.

Mr. Thomas: Oh.

Afternote:

The elderly couple survived with no issues, the bank gave them a vacation as a reward to Panama City, Florida. The older gentleman had several small but non-life-threatening heart attacks, while enjoying the view of other beach goers.

Damnation Recommendation:

Initial recommendation for Thomas Nathan Thomas, after the soul spends ten-thousand years as child size chew toy for Cerberus' puppies (standard child abuse damnation), is that the soul be moved to the demon sound recording studio and be fed to the scarab beetles and screams recorded, with soul review in one-thousand years.

DOCUMENT 4

INTERVIEW: 199449T6R

Interview: I99449t6r

Demon: Bill-98986569I-99887666*e4

Soul

Given Name: William George McDonald

Also Known as: Georgie

Occupation: None

Transcribed by: Demon Transcriber #09079878767653457a3b

Transcript

Bill-98986569I-99887666*e4 (From here on referred to as "Bill") It is my job to interview you to determine your damnation status and/or clarification of specifics of your level of damnation in hell.

William George McDonald (From here on referred to as "Mr. McDonald".): What in the Flying Fuck am I doing here?

Bill: Sir, I would not suggest you say, "Flying Fuck", we have these, well pests, that like to come around when you say those words.

Mr. McDonald: I will say whatever I want, it's a free fucking country.

(Behind Mr. McDonald a roughly seven-inch phallus with wings, comes through the wall, Mr. McDonald does not notice.)

Bill: No this is Hell, and it is anything but a free country, I am here to interview you so we can determine your damnation correctly.

Mr. McDonald: I don't give a flying fuck what you're here for.

(Another larger phallus with wings appears behind Mr. McDonald.)

Bill: I have warned you that your actions may have consequences; I have also attempted to begin the interview. If you do not adjust your attitude, we may have to take a break and allow your actions to dictate your consequences.

Mr. McDonald: I told you once you ugly fucker, I don't give a flying fuck about you, a flying fuck about this interview, a flying fuck about Hell, and I really don't give a flying fuck that you don't want me to say flying fuck. Just for you, flying fuck, flying fuck, flying fuck, flying fuck, flying fuck, flying fuck, flying fuck, flying fuck, and a gigantic flying fuck for you.

(Behind Mr. McDonald, winged phalluses of all sizes started to appear; one reddish phallus appeared at the end, roughly the size of a medium fire extinguisher.)

Bill: Sir, I must say that you are going to start your damnation off, like a gang bang.

(Bill, gesturing towards Mr. McDonald, cuffs with chains leading to the opposite side of the table from Mr. McDonald appeared on the wrist. Ankle cuffs also appeared on Mr. McDonald locking his feet in place. The chains on the wrist began to pull Mr. McDonald across the table, pulling him to his feet and laying him across the table.)

Bill: Sir, I am going to take a little vacation while you deal with your own flying fucks, I will return in a month or five to check on you.

(Bill walked through the wall opposite from Mr. McDonald. The winged phalluses began to grow larger and moved faster.)

Interview stopped for eight months and four days.

(Bill walks in through a wall, wearing a Hawaiian shirt and lei. He examines the chair across from Mr. McDonald, it is completely covered with blood and multiple other fluids. He gestures to the chair and table. The chair, table, and his half the room are clean.)

Bill: Sir, now that I have had a short vacation, I will begin the interview again. Are you ready to be civil and answer my questions?

(Mr. McDonald is unable to speak at this time. Bill looks at Mr. McDonald, gestures and three of the pests remove themselves from Mr. McDonald's mouth.)

Mr. McDonald: I will be nice. I promise I will be nice…please I will be nice.

Document 4 Interview: I99449t6r

(Two of the pests shoot back into Mr. McDonald's mouth.)

Bill: I will never be able to complete this interview with all of these around. I will do something about them if you promise to conduct yourself in a polite manner.

(Mr. McDonald shakes his head vigorously up and down indicating agreement, Bill makes a gesture and the winged phalluses begin removing themselves from Mr. McDonald's orifices and flying out of the room through the wall behind Mr. McDonald. Bill does not remove the chains or cuffs.)

Bill: Now Please state your full name.

(The fire extinguisher size winged phallus currently is working its way out of Mr. McDonald's anus.)

Mr. McDonald: William George McDonald, but most people call me Georgie.

Bill: Mr. McDonald you died on Friday, September I4th, 200I. Three days after the September IIth, attacks on the world trade center in New York City.

Mr. McDonald: I guess, I don't remember much, I was celebrating.

Bill: Usually we don't care about earthly dates unless it has a direct effect on the death, or reasons for the death. To clarify, you were celebrating the attack?

Document 4 Interview: I99449t6r

Mr. McDonald: God yes, it was time someone took down those celebrations of capitalism.

Bill: As I understand it you hate capitalism.

Mr. McDonald: Fuc…ah….you see.. I hate capitalism; I am a devoted socialist, the only true fair government.

Bill: On the day you died, you decide to show someone, or a group, how happy you were that the attack happened. Is that correct so far?

Mr. McDonald: Yeah, I had just got some of my money, and was celebrating, I wanted to show the capitalist slimes that it was a good thing.

Bill: Just to clarify, where did you get the money from?

Mr. McDonald: I had some money coming to me.

Bill: Mr. McDonald, if you cannot tell me, I am sure that the pests would love to return, and I could use another vacation.

Mr. McDonald: What does it matter? I got money ok.

Bill: Answer the question or don't, I will not mind another vacation.

Mr. McDonald: My grandmother gave it to me.

Bill: She gave it to you?

Mr. McDonald: I stole it out of her purse, while she slept.

Bill: You snuck into your grandmother's house and stole her food money?

Mr. McDonald: Yep she has a ton of money that she doesn't share, Grandpa made from his business, damn capitalist.

Bill: You took your stolen money and then what happened?

Mr. McDonald: I went shopping; I wanted the new XBOX, and a few other things.

Bill: You took your stolen Capitalist money and went shopping for the newest Capitalist inventions, sounds like a good Socialist me too.

Mr. McDonald: It's not like that, I mean everyone has one why not me.

(Bill reaches out to Mr. McDonald who is still strapped across the table, pulls back on his head and smashes it into the table, the head is nothing, but pieces of bone and brain scattered over the table.)

Bill: I hate idiots.

(Bill gestures, Mr. McDonald's head begins healing.)

Bill: After you went shopping, what did you do?

Mr. McDonald: Well there is the biker bar, the "Panhead Alley", down by where I live. They are always riding those Harleys up and down the road, do you know that Harley is like the symbol for Capitalism, I hate 'em.

Bill: I don't have all day. Stick to the information I am asking. What did you do?

Mr. McDonald: I went and got me some vodka, good old Communist vodka, and I drank the entire bottle.

Bill: You drank a shot and half, no more.

Mr. McDonald: It must have been strong because I decided to tell those bikers exactly what I felt about their country.

Bill: How did you do that?

Mr. McDonald: I marched into the Panhead Alley, took my stand on Capitalism.

Bill: How did you take your stand on Capitalism?

Mr. McDonald: Well I marched right in. I saw they had a flag on the wall. I walked right up to it and ripped it down. Yelled at the top of my lungs, "you all deserved to be attacked, those Capitalist fuckers deserved to die, I am gonna take this flag and wipe my ass with it".

Bill: Do you remember anything else?

Mr. McDonald: I do but I don't think it is right. I remember a nametag, it said "Bull" coming from behind the bar, and I remember a gorilla grabbing me by the throat. Wait I remember, someone hit me with what felt like a baseball bat.

Document 4 Interview: I99449t6r

Bill: You went into a biker bar three days after, September IIth, and ripped down a flag, and told them they deserved to be attacked, then told them you were "gonna wipe your ass" with the flag. Is that correct?

Mr. McDonald: Yeah, that's right.

Bill: That is everything we need to know.

Mr. McDonald: How does knowing that stuff help you determine how my damnation is?

Bill: Actually, it has nothing to do with your damnation, we just didn't believe you were stupid enough to walk into a biker bar and do that. You proved us wrong.

Afternote:

Mr. McDonald was taken by "Bull", "Gorilla," and "Tiny," he was not hit by a baseball bat, that was Bull's fist. Mr. McDonald was taken to the highway and other than the moderate damage done while restraining him, released unhurt. Where he walked into a truck moving new XBOX's to the store. The Flag was returned to the owner of the bar.

Damnation Recommendation:

Recommend that the soul live in an eight by eight room, with only Socialist produced products for five-hundred years, followed by only Communist products for five-hundred years. Damnation review in one-thousand years.

Damnation adjustment:

Mr. McDonald could not find any Socialist products. An adjustment was made with the addition of a video feed of Capitalist products via QVC and home shopping network will be added. He will be allowed to order but orders will never go through.

DOCUMENT 5

INTERVIEW: 123D5768S

Interview: I23d5768s

Demon: Jack-989865691—86196634*e4

Soul

Given Name: Barry Bo Metheny

Also Known as: Unknown

Occupation: Rapist

Transcribed by: Demon Transcriber #09079878767653457a3b

Transcript

Jack-989865691-86196634*e4 (From here on referred to as "Jack".): It is my job to interview you to determine your damnation status and/or clarification of specifics of your level of damnation in Hell.

Barry Bo Metheny (From here on referred to as "Mr. Metheny".): Excuse me could you repeat that, I could have sworn you said, "determine my damnation status".

Jack: Yes, I am doing this interview to determine your damnation status for your internment into Hell.

Mr. Metheny: Wait there must be some kind of mistake, I go to church, I give money to charity, I live a good life.

Jack: Can you please state your full name?

Mr. Metheny: Don't I get a lawyer, a representative of some kind, I don't deserve Hell.

(Jack conjures two Pears of Anguish, one appearing in Mr. Metheny's mouth.)

Jack: I will state this again, you are in Hell with a capital "H", you will notice I just put a Pear of Anguish in your mouth and another in your anus. If you are not familiar with them, they are from the I600's; they can be expanded by turning the key that is sticking out. Hear let me demonstrate.

(Jack waves his hand, the key sticking from the mouth, turns one full turn. Mr. Metheny makes a muffled scream.)

Jack: You are a serial rapist, we know about the babysitters, we know about your secretary, we know about the girls in college, we know everything.

(Jack waves his hand the keys do another full turn, Mr. Metheny screams a louder muffled scream.)

Jack: We know that you are a rapist; there is no question why you should be here. I am here to just clarify a few things about the day you died.

(Jack looks at his wrist, no watch resides there.)

Jack: I think it is time I took a break. Hope you like barbecue.

(Jack waves his hand as he walks through the wall
away from Mr. Metheny. Behind Mr. Metheny, a
Brazen Bull appears, with the side door open. Mr.
Metheny floats up, then into the Brazen Bull, the
door closes and locks. A fire starts under the
copper bull belly beginning the slow boiling of
Mr. Metheny. Smoke begins coming out of the bull's
nostrils. Mr. Metheny begins screaming.)

Interview stops for nine months four days

(Jack enters from the wall he walked out of,
carrying several white takeout boxes. He gestures
toward the Brazen Bull. Mr. Metheny's smoked body
comes out of the Brazen Bull, and into the chair
opposite Jack. Straps go around Mr. Metheny's
wrist and ankles. The Pear of Anguish in his mouth
disappears, the other does not.)

Jack: Now to continue the interview. Please state
your full name.

(Jack opens one of the takeout boxes, it is filled
with pork ribs the smell fills the room. Kansas
City is emblazoned on the top of the container.)

Mr. Metheny: Barry, I am Barry Bo Metheny.

Jack: Mr. Metheny as I have already said we know
you are a rapist. We are here just to clarify some
points so we can give you the best damnation
experience possible. The questions have to do with
the night you died. Do you remember that night?

Mr. Metheny: Don't I get a lawyer?

(Jack waves his hand, the sound of the Pear of
Anguish key spinning can be heard, along with the
snap of it expanding. Mr. Metheny screams, then
begins to sob. Jack begins viciously tearing into
ribs like a true carnivore.)

Jack: We pave the roads of Hell with lawyers; it
is the only use we could find for them. No, you do
not get representation this is Hell, not a
Democracy or a Republic. Now do you remember that
night?

Mr. Metheny: What about a deal with the Devil, I
will give anything.

(All that is left is the bones of the ribs, every
scrap of meat that was on the ribs has been
devoured, he closes the box and opens a box with
Texas emblazoned on the lid. Beef Brisket fills
the container, Jack smiles and picks up a large
piece.)

Jack: You have nothing we want. We have your soul,
you were at best a mediocre lower middleman, you
have nothing of value. We, the minions of Hell,
are here to carry out your damnation. Do you
remember that night?

(A phone appears on the desk. It rings and Jack
picks it up.)

Jack into the phone: Jack-989865691—86196634*e4,
yes, yes sir he did, I see sir, yes sir, No
inconvenience at all sir, thank you sir.

(Jack hangs up the phone)

Jack: You invoked the Devil's name, now he has taken an interest in you, I will speak to you in five-thousand Years, wherein we will continue this interview.

(Jack picks up his boxes still full of barbecue and walks out of the room. Mr. Metheny rises and begins floating towards a wall. A three-foot hole opens on the wall. The Hellfire comes through around the edges, a large red hand comes through the hole and pulls Mr. Metheny into the hole.)

Interview stops for 5000 years and one day

(Mr. Metheny drops from the ceiling into the interview chair, wrist and ankle cuffs appear locking him into the chair, every inch of his body is crisp. Jack enters and sits. He is still carrying two takeout boxes.)

Jack: I hope you enjoyed our little break, I did. Do you know that barbecue is different everywhere you go? Three of the best things about your world, Texas brisket, Kansas City pork ribs and Carolina pulled pork sandwich.

Mr. Metheny: I was burned for five, five thousand years. I was forced to count and keep track of the days. They made me repeat each day I forgot to count. How is that possible? How is there barbecue still in the world after five-thousand years?

Jack: Time means nothing down here we control everything, including time.

(Jack opens the brisket take out box and begins to eat.)

Mr. Metheny: At least that time counts toward my damnation, every little bit will help.

Jack: It counts for nothing, that was just my Lord's whim.

(Mr. Metheny begins sobbing.)

Jack: Now to continue the interview, do you remember the night you were killed?

Mr. Metheny: That was so long ago.

Jack: Are you saying you refuse to answer?

Mr. Metheny: No, no, just taking a moment to remember. I believe I remember that night. I needed to work late. I asked the new intern to stay late to help.

(Jack's prehensile tail shoots out hitting Mr. Matheny in the groin, goes up through the body, into the head, out one eye in the other eye and out the mouth. The tail then begins to shake. Destroying Mr. Metheny's body. Jack's tail retracts, he waves his hand, and Mr. Matheny heals back to the previous state.

Jack: Lie to me again and I will have to take action to punish you.

Mr. Metheny: But you have boiled me alive, and destroyed my body…that's not punishment?

Jack: No that is just motivation, now do you remember that night?

Mr. Metheny: Yes, I remember.

Jack: Tell me what you remember.

Mr. Metheny: I had finished my work early, but I saw the new intern. She looked like an easy piece. I made up that I needed to work late and asked if she could be the one to stay with me.

Jack: That is more accurate, when did you decide to rape her?

Mr. Metheny: As soon as I saw her, I was coming into the building that morning. I smiled at her, she ignored me, can you believe it she ignored me. What a bitch.

Jack: Is that why you decided to rape her because she ignored you?

Mr. Metheny: Yes, and she looked so hot, like she wanted it.

(Jack reaches out, and smacks Mr. Metheny's head off, it rolls to the wall and bounces off. The head floats back to the body. Jack heals Mr. Metheny's head.)

Mr. Metheny: What did I do?

Jack: Just you being you, now back to the interview.

Mr. Metheny: What do you mean, just being me?

Jack: You are a major asshat. But I do not have time or inclination to explain it to you. How did you proceed?

Mr. Metheny: Uh …I…. uh.

Jack: If you do not answer I will be forced to take another break.

(Mr. Metheny whimpers, and makes a small sob.)

Mr. Metheny: I checked to see if she had signed the company's anti-gun policy. I didn't want to take the chance she had a gun. Those things are dangerous.

Jack: Yes, guns can be dangerous to people like you. After you checked the policy, how did you proceed?

Mr. Metheny: It was after everyone else in the office had left, I asked her to get the box of files and come to my office. The box was so she would have her hands full and I could get the advantage.

Jack: I take it she got the box of files and came to your office.

Mr. Metheny: Yeah, I went behind the door. I had a set of handcuffs that I have used before, they came in handy to secure them.

Jack: You are behind the door with the handcuffs, then what happened?

Mr. Metheny: She walked through the door, I reached out and grabbed her by the throat, and left wrist. She dropped the box, the files scattered on the floor. I remember thinking I will make her refile that box.

Jack: You had her by the throat and left wrist, is that correct?

Mr. Metheny: I must have missed her wrist. I didn't have a hold of her. I remember my left hand was in pain. I looked at my left hand, and it was not where it should have been, it was reversed.

Jack: She broke your left hand. Can you remember what happened next?

Mr. Metheny: I was looking at my deformed hand, wondering how that happened. She must have spun to the right. She locked my arm in some funky way. I was thinking how I was gonna explain this to H.R. and how it went against company policy.

Jack: In your attempt to rape the intern, she broke your left wrist, and wrapped your right arm in a lock position? You were not very good at this were you? Rhetorical question do not answer that. Do you remember what happened next?

Mr. Metheny: I think I ended upside-down on my head. I could see, wait, I could see my own ass? I don't remember anything else.

Jack: We have enough, normally I would have already sent you to your damnation but I wanted to enlighten you to a few pieces of information, because you should know how much of a failure you really are. Your intern did not see you in the morning, you were never important enough to really be noticed. When you looked to see if she signed the company firearm policy, you should have reviewed her resume. You would have noticed she is a Krav Maga instructor in her spare time. In fact, when she was hired, she offered to teach self-defense to anyone in the company that wanted it for free.

Mr. Metheny: What?

Jack: I am about to break our company policy, but this is Hell they don't really care. Rapist damnation is a standard here in Hell, you will be sent to the pig rape arena.

Mr. Metheny: I am not gonna rape a pig.

Jack: Who said anything about YOU raping?

Afternote:

The intern attempted to disable Mr. Metheny, by using her leg for leverage on an arm lock. In her excitement, she snapped his neck and repositioned his head so that his own buttocks were in his own view.

Damnation Recommendation:

Recommend the standard damnation for rape, Pig Rape Arena, alternating with Horse Rape Arena bi-annually. Recommend peer review daily. Recommend damnation review in ten-thousand years.

Damnation adjustment:

During the evenings when the rape arenas are not as busy, Mr. Metheny will become an inanimate practice dummy for anti-rape classes. He will not be able to move but will feel every hit fully.

DOCUMENT 6

INTERVIEW: 7899630-O9

Interview: 7899630-o9

Demon: Nick-99887554-7789009*e4

Soul

Given Name: Fabio Alexander Lensky

Also Known as: Fabs

Occupation: Mugger/Thief

Transcribed by: Demon Transcriber #0907987876765-3457a3b

Transcript

Nick-99887554-7789009*e4 (From here on referred to as "Nick".): It is my job to interview you to determine your damnation status and/or clarification of specifics of your level of damnation in Hell.

Fabio Alexander Lensky (From here on referred to as "Mr. Lensky".): What do you mean like the TV show Lucifer? Those demons are hot!

Nick: Please state your full name.

Mr. Lensky: Where is that hot demon Maize? Man, what I wouldn't give to spend a night with her.

Nick: Usually we ignore requests, but I think I can help you with this one.

(Nick reaches and a phone appears)

Nick: Yes, this is demon Nick-99887554-7789009*e4, the soul has requested a night with Mazzikeen. She's on her way, thank you.

Mr Lensky: You mean Maize is on her way?

(A short female demon appears; she has ogre like tusks, and a studded three-foot club.)

Nick: You may have wanted to know a little more about Mazzikeen before you made that request. She is actually a demon from the Jewish belief system. She knows of your family's support of the Nazi treatment of Jewish people during World War II. She also knows of your own personal semi-worship of Nazis and their uniforms. She would like to have a chat with you regarding that support.

(Mazzikeen's tail reaches Mr. Lensky's neck and wraps around it. Picking him up above her horned head.)

Mazzikeen: I will have him back in the morning.

(Mazzikeen and Mr. Lensky disappear.)

Interview stopped for one day

(Mazzikeen appears with Mr. Lensky held by the ankle. Mr. Lensky is wearing a fuzzy pink see through bathrobe, fuzzy pink handcuffs, and pink ball gag. Mazzikeen drops Mr. Lensky on top of the interview chair, and the ball gag disappears.)

Mazzikeen: Man, I love that show Lucifer, I get so many requests now that it is on TV. I owe you one Nick.

(Mazzikeen disappears.)

Nick: Now that you have had your request, can you state your name.

Mr. Lensky: She, she, she used the club, over and over. She had sand, salt and Tiger balm mixed as lube. Oh god the club.

(Mr. Lensky begins crying into his own shoulder.)

Nick: State your name.

Mr. Lensky: Fabio Alexander Lensky, but you can call me Fabs.

Nick: No, I will not. Mr. Lensky we are here to answer some questions about the day you died. On that day, you attempted to rob a woman. What can you tell me about what happened on that evening?

Mr. Lensky: I had just moved from San Diego to Fort Worth. I had one of those week to week places. I could not believe how trusting people were in Fort Worth, they left everything out for anyone to steal. It was easy but I just wasn't getting enough to pay the next week.

Nick: Go on.

Mr. Lensky: It was Sunday, and my rent was due on Monday, I saw all these people going to church on Sunday morning. They kept talking about going to a place called the Stock Yards. I don't know what that is but man they had some money.

Nick: As I understand, it was Sunday and church was over?

Mr. Lensky: Yeah, they all came out of this big church. Man, lots of them were dressed up like cowboys. I kept wondering where the horses and guns were.

Nick: I wonder where they were.

Mr. Lensky: I saw a perfect target, this woman was wearing this thing from the 70s, and it was like a three-piece suit but pink and for a woman. Somehow, she squeezed her oversized breasts into it. I never saw anything like that in San Diego. Oh, her hair, she had it teased up almost a foot above her head. Then I saw it, that fashion disaster had a Coach purse, a real Coach purse in the middle of this fashion desert.

Nick: So, you choose her because of her purse?

Mr. Lensky: Yep, that is actually how I got my nickname "Fabs" 'cause I knew what fashion things were worth money. All I had to do was grab that purse and get away. She was walking to her truck. Would you believe she drove a truck that you had to climb into. I didn't know how I was gonna grab that purse; but then luck was on my side.

Nick: How was luck on your side?

Mr. Lensky: She went to her truck, then turned around and headed for the church. I decided to jump in the back of the truck and wait until there was some privacy, I was thinking I might even get more than her purse.

Nick: Your plan was to get to a place with more privacy?

Mr. Lensky: Yeah, I went around the other side of the truck, and climbed in the back. I almost fell, the truck was so high. I crawled up near the cab and waited. I heard her talking as she came back. I heard her say something like "the higher the hair, the closer to Jesus" and something about "tubing down the Guadalupe". Still not sure what the hell she was talking about.

Nick: You crawled in the back of the truck. I take it you decided to ride with her to a place with more privacy.

Mr. Lensky: Yeah, I looked to make sure she was alone and, then just laid down for the ride.

Nick: How did that go?

Mr. Lensky: Well it started out okay, she went to a place called Whataburger, and that was a little scary. There were men in the parking lot wearing guns on their hips, I mean they weren't even trying to hiding them.

Nick: Whataburger, I will make a specific note on that.

Mr. Lensky: Then as we were leaving, she yelled something about "Waylon and Willie" out to some of the guys in the parking lot. That is when it got a little rough.

Nick: How did it get rough?

Mr. Lensky: I am not exactly sure what happened, she started driving wild, she drove over something, might have been a curb, and went on a side road, I don't think she hit the brakes once. I could hear her singing something about "don't touch my willie". I didn't think that there were a lot of trans people in Texas.

Nick: First there are a few, and that is a famous song.

Mr. Lensky: It's a song? Odd song, I was getting beat up in the back of that truck. I almost died there.

Nick: Stop whining so much, you just got a few little bruises. Now continue.

Mr. Lensky: After what felt like a hundred miles, we finally stopped at what looked like a shack, it was in the middle of nowhere. It was a perfect spot. Nobody was around for miles. I was gonna get that purse and her truck and whatever else I wanted.

Nick: You found your privacy you were looking for. How did you proceed?

Mr. Lensky: She went into the shack, I dropped down off the side of the truck, I had the drop on her. My friends in Cali had warned me about those Texans and their guns. I was ready for that, I grabbed her purse, so she couldn't pull the gun out of there. I scared her; I knew it. Then the funniest thing happened. She looked at me and said, "Well bless your heart." I don't know what she meant by that.

Nick: You had the purse. Did you try to leave?

Mr. Lensky: I was gonna, but I wanted that jewelry she was wearing, it was big and gaudy but it looked like real gold. She was just standing there, looking at me. I opened that purse but no gun. I guessed she didn't have one. She was still just standing there. She says "I got something to show you", she starts unbuttoning her blouse.

Nick: Do you remember what happened next?

Mr. Lensky: She didn't have much taste in clothes, but she did have a body with all the curves in the right spot. I couldn't wait to see how big those breasts really were. She is unbuttoning slowly, very slowly, god it was driving me nuts.

Nick: Did she continue to unbutton the blouse?

Mr. Lensky: She unbuttoned all of it. I could see the beginning of her bra. I was so excited…I really didn't think Texas women were this wild.

Nick: I wouldn't know anything about that, but we get every sort down here.

Mr. Lensky: All I could see was the opening of that blouse. It was mesmerizing. Then I saw a... I think I saw, it was a gun hanging from her bra. What the fuck was that?

Nick: Is that all you remember?

Mr. Lensky: I remember a bang.

Nick: That would be the end of your life.

Damnation Recommendation:

Recommend walking across Texas East to West and back, while wearing a "Willie Nelson sucks" shirt. Only able to get water from people who believe the best brisket is in New York. Recommend damnation review in one-thousand years.

Damnation Adjustment:

Mazzikeen has requested when the damned soul reaches either border that she is given him for a day to help with the damnation.

DOCUMENT 7

INTERVIEW: 7786654-O9E5

Interview: 7786654-o9e5

Demon: Bob-998754-7579s77*e4

Soul

Given Name: Terry Howard Carter

Also Known as: None

Occupation: Drug dealer

Transcribed by: Demon Transcriber #09079878767653457a3b

Transcript

Bob-998754-7579s77*e4: (From here on referred to as "Bob".): It is my job to interview you to determine your damnation status and/or clarification of specifics of your level of damnation in Hell.

Terry Howard Carter: (From here on referred to as "Mr. Carter."): Wait, what?

Bob: I will say again, it is my job to interview you to determine your damnation status and/or clarification of specifics of your level of damnation in Hell. Please state your full name.

Mr. Carter: Wait, what are you talking about, Hell doesn't exist, it's just made up stuff.

Bob: Please state your full name now.

Mr. Carter: Whatever, Terry is my name.

Bob: I said your full name, seems like you will need some motivation to comply.

(Bob waves his hand and a small brownish 14lb dog appeared, it was a corgi mix and was wagging its hind part to wag the short tail. It had a spiked collar on.)

Mr. Carter: Oh, what a cute puppy, wait why are you torturing this poor puppy. Collars are just torture devices; they do not make them look cute. I bet you dress this cute puppy up on Halloween.

(Mr. Carter reaches down for the collar. The dog's head grows quickly to the size of a hippopotamus head, and snaps at Mr. Carter's left forearm taking it off at the elbow.)

Bob: Here we have one of my favorite hounds, his name is Mr. Tinkles.

(Mr. Carter is looking from the stub of his arm to the now small Mr. Tinkles.)

Mr. Carter: But I was kind to animals, I was in P.E.T.A., I protected them.

Bob: Mr. Tinkles would disagree with you.

(Mr. Carter looked down at his stub.)

Mr. Carter: Oh god I'm going to die, can you please call 9II! Please I don't want to die!

Bob: I have some news you may be interested in.

(Mr. Tinkles starts bouncing on its hind legs, trying to get Bob's attention.)

Bob: Okay, Mr. Tinkles you can have the play toy.

(Mr. Tinkles bounces and does a backflip, then jumps directly at Mr. Carter. Mr. Tinkles grows to the size of a small bull. The dog grabs Mr. Carter and begins to shake him back and forth like a rag doll.)

Bob: Mr. Tinkles, sit.

(Mr. Tinkles stops, reduces to the smaller size, sits with Mr. Carter's leg still in its mouth. Bob waves and Mr. Carter is healed to the point of just having his arm bitten off.)

Mr. Carter: ...wh...wh...what did you do to this poor dog......why are you mistreating them....

Bob: What do you mean "them?"

Mr. Carter: I don't want to assume their gender, that would be wrong.

Bob: I don't think you will have to worry about that anytime soon. Mr. Tinkles would you like a friend to play with?

(Mr. Tinkles bounces and does a backflip, carrying Mr. Carter with him, smacking him into the ceiling, wall, and then the floor.)

Bob: What a good boy, oh Rufus.

(A small 12lb white and black terrier mix dog appears, wearing a chain collar.)

Bob: This is Mr. Tinkles friend Rufus. They love to play together. Mr. Tinkles, Roof, play toy time.

(Rufus grabs Mr. Carter's arm, and Mr. Tinkles has the leg, they proceed to use Mr. Carter as a pull toy, all the while bouncing off the walls, and ceiling. Bob conjures a bottle of Jameson Irish whiskey, a tumbler, a Pipe and Tobacco pouch, proceeds to drink, and smoke. Bob enjoys the show for the next few hours, finishing half the bottle while watching Mr. Tinkle and Rufus play.)

Bob: Mr. Tinkles, sit. Rufus, sit.

(Both dogs quickly assume a sitting position, each beside Bob. The bits of Mr. Carter's body slowly move back together, healing to the point where only the stub of an arm is not attached. He has small chew marks all over his body.)

Mr. Carter: Why…

Bob: The little ones need exercise too, I mean it would not be right to keep them cooped up all day, and since you needed a little example of what can be done it all works out for the better. Now state your full name.

(Mr. Carter nervously looks from Mr. Tinkles to Rufus back to Mr. Tinkles.)

Mr. Carter: Terry Howard Carter

Document 7 Interview: 7786654-o9e5

Bob: See that was not that hard to answer. We need to get some information about the days leading up to your death and the day you died. Are you going to answer my questions?

(Mr. Carter looks at Mr. Tinkles who is now chewing what looks like a hand. Mr. Carter makes a whining noise.)

Mr. Carter: I will answer anything you want. Can I ask a question first?

Bob: You just did, but what is your question?

Mr. Carter: Where am I?

Bob: Remember that information I said you may be interested in, you are dead, you have been damned to Hell, and we are gathering some information to ensure your damnation is efficient and effective. We aim to please.

Mr. Carter: You mean all that stuff my grandma was telling me all the time is real?

Bob: Not exactly, it's real for her. You have your own special Hell. We go out of our way to tailor your damnation especially for you. We are givers that way.

Mr. Carter: Shit, it's real.

Bob: Mr. Carter, yes, we have covered that. Now, let us talk about the days leading up to your death. You were in Colorado Springs, what were you doing there.

Mr. Carter: I was grabbing some stuff to sell in Kansas, that's where I am from.

Bob: Be specific what "stuff."

Mr. Carter: Colorado Tumbleweed.

Bob: You mean Marijuana.

Mr. Carter: Yeah dumbass Weed, Mary Jane, Cannabis, Reefer, the Devil's Weed, Something to Blaze, Dope, yes Marijuana.

Bob: Hounds, sic' em!

(Mr. Tinkles and Rufus jumped to each side of Mr. Carter's face ripping and chewing in the way only hellhounds can rip and chew. As both dogs worked their way down the body, the upper portion healed while the other portion was being ripped and chewed. During this time Bob finished the bottle of whiskey and smoked his pipe. When the bottle is empty Bob conjures another bottle.)

Bob: Hounds, sit.

(The dogs take their position on either side of Bob. Mr. Carter continues to heal until he is partially together, Still missing the arm and covered in chew and rip wounds.)

Mr. Carter: Sorry, I'm sorry, I am sorry I was an asshole.

Bob: See how simple it is, back to the interview. So why were you in Colorado Springs?

Mr. Carter: I was there buying marijuana to resell in Kansas, where it is illegal. Wait is that why I am in Hell because I sold drugs.

Bob: Mr. Carter you are not in Hell because you sold drugs, you are in Hell because you are a lying, backstabbing, piece of garbage who didn't do a single kind thing in your life. That part is not in question, we have other questions. You never made it back to Kansas. What happened?

Mr. Carter: There was this fine chick…

(Mr. Tinkles growled.)

Mr. Carter: I met a young lady. She was there, waiting on some of the old women, she was planning on throwing paint on the furs they wore.

Bob: Is this something you do often?

Mr. Carter: Oh yeah, it's one of my favorite things to do, you find these old women, get a bucket and throw or spray red paint on them. They're murderers, what do they expect?

Bob: You became associated with this young lady?

Mr. Carter: Uh?

Bob: You got to know here?

Mr. Carter: I got to know more of her if you know what I mean.

Bob: Stick to the questions I am asking, or I will open my bottle and let the dogs play some more.

Document 7 Interview: 7786654-o9e5

(Mr. Carter looks from Mr. Tinkles to Rufus and back to Mr. Tinkles then begins sweating.)

Mr. Carter: Yes, I got to know her.

Bob: Did you and her throw paint on the ladies?

Mr. Carter: No, it was August, none of them were wearing furs.

Bob: But something else happened, correct?

Mr. Carter: Yeah, we had just finished a doobie, and we were filling up on gas for the ride to Kansas, when this bunch of bikers pulled in beside us.

Bob: Go on.

Mr. Carter: Well Chris, her name was Christina, started yelling at the bikers, they were wearing leather, man it took me two joints to calm her down. Then she goes on and on about the leather and the beautiful cows. She says we should have thrown paint on them. She was my piece, so I had to agree with her. She goes "there were a bunch of them, I wonder where they were going?" I didn't know, but she was on a roll.

Bob: She wanted to throw paint on the leather they were wearing. Did that sound dangerous to you?

Mr. Carter: Naw man, you throw the paint and the run, and if they call the cops it's usually a misdemeanor, with a few days in jail. Nothing I can't handle.

(Bob is blank, just staring at Mr. Carter for 30 to 40 seconds. Mr. Tinkles looks at Stephen with a "what the fuck look", Stephen just shakes his head side to side, and does a doggy shrug.)

Bob: Okay, I am beginning to get the picture.

Mr. Carter: Chris grabs her phone and is really intense for a few…, to be honest I don't know how long because the two joints were really hitting.

Bob: What else do you remember?

Mr. Carter: I woke up; I guess I passed out. We were on the road in my van, but we were going the wrong way. We are going north on 75 instead of east on 70, I'm not stupid, I have done the drive a few times.

Bob: I am not sure you are correct on that statement but go on.

Mr. Carter: What statement?

Bob: The Statement "I'm not stupid"

Mr. Carter: uh?

Bob: Just go on.

Mr. Carter: I know the road we were supposed to be on. Chris looks over at me and says she had a great idea. She says she knows where the bikers are going. I was pissed but she kept me happy, so I kept my cool. I asked where they were going?

Bob: Did she have an answer?

Mr. Carter: She said "Sturgis, South Dakota," some kind of biker party. She had this idea, find the bikers from the gas station, or if we can't find them some other bikers will work as long as they are wearing leather. Cover them in red paint and run like hell. The way she had it figured, we could be going before the bikers knew what hit them. We may have to spend a few nights in jail, but as she said it would be worth it to teach them a lesson for wearing leather.

(Mr. Tinkles cocked his head to the side staring at Mr. Carter.)

Bob: This sounds like a great idea, can you continue?

Mr. Carter: It was a great idea, and she said that once we did this, she was gonna give me some.

Bob: You mean some more?

Mr. Carter: Well to be honest, we never really did anything, we smoked a lot of my stash, but we never seemed to get it on, but man was she willing.

Bob: Let me get the facts correct, you were driving north, chasing bikers to throw paint…

Mr. Carter: Red paint, it must be red for the blood of the animals.

Bob: To throw red paint on them, because afterwards you are going to get some from "Chris".

Mr. Carter: No man, it was a good idea, the get some was just a bonus.

Bob: Got it, so what happened?

Mr. Carter: We drove for hours. All we saw were bikes but not the ones we wanted. It was cool though, Chris flashed me her boobs a few times.

Bob: You, got to see her breasts?

Mr. Carter: It was just a promise of what was to come. We were about to give up finding the bikers from the gas station when Chris saw them. They were going into one of those, what do you call them, places where you stop to rest?

Bob: A rest stop?

Mr. Carter: Yeah, this one was called the Deadwood Creek resting area. I turned the van into the rest stop, just in time. We stayed away from them while we made our plans.

Bob: What was your plan?

Mr. Carter: Chris was gonna go around the other side with the van and park it. I was gonna take a bucket of paint and sneak closer to them. Chris was supposed to distract them somehow and I would throw the paint while they were trying to figure out what happened. Then we run to the van and take off.

Bob: Seems simple enough, how did it go?

Mr. Carter: I don't really know. I mean I took the bucket and snuck around behind them. Chris took the van to the other side.

Bob: The van full marijuana?

Mr. Carter: Yeah, my van, she went to the other side. I got as close as I could. I was waiting, but nothing happened, I waited some more, but nothing.

Bob: Could you see Chris?

Mr. Carter: You know what, I couldn't see her, she went around the corner beyond the bikers.

Bob: Would that be the road to the exit to the rest stop

Mr. Carter: Yeah, so we could get away fast.

Bob: Did the distraction ever come?

Mr. Carter: I must have missed it, but I couldn't wait anymore. They were getting on their bikes, they were gonna get away.

Bob: You had to act before they got away?

Mr. Carter: Yeah, I ran towards them, took my bucket and threw the paint.

Bob: Did you throw the paint on the leather?

Mr. Carter: I missed.

Bob: Did you hit their bikes?

Mr. Carter: I missed those too.

Document 7 Interview: 7786654-o9e5

Bob: What did you hit?

Mr. Carter: The sidewalk.

Bob: You missed the bikers wearing leather, you missed the motorcycles they were riding, and you hit the sidewalk.

Mr. Carter: I did get a little on the boot of one of them.

Bob: How did the bikers react?

Mr. Carter: Not well.

Bob: I bet. Can you be more specific?

Mr. Carter: Bikers wear a lot of skull rings. I did not realize that.

Bob: I can see that from the skull impressions still on your face. Is that all that happened?

Mr. Carter: The one that I got paint on his boot showed it to me, then he took a chain and hooked it to my leg, then his bike.

Bob: Did he ride away.

Mr. Carter: He rode around the parking lot first, and then he rode off. I don't remember anything after that.

Bob: That is because you died.

Mr. Carter: Can you tell me what happened to Chris?

Bob: I am not supposed to, rules you understand, but I will break them for this. Chris took your van full of marijuana and sold it during the bike rally in Sturgis, South Dakota. Chris ended up getting with the biker that pulled you around the parking lot. She is now a pass around for him and his friends. She also ended up giving him the money from selling your marijuana and your van. She also wears a lot of leather now.

Damnation Recommendation:

Recommend increasing the soul's intelligence. Repeat the last eight hours of his life unable to change anything, skip the "boobie" flashes. Damnation review in five-hundred years.

DOCUMENT 8

INTERVIEW: 3445657-UJY5

Interview: 3445657-ujy5

Demon: Fred-8765439-7844*e4

<u>Soul</u>

Given Name: John Robert Jonnas

Also Known as: JoJo

Occupation: Thief

Transcribed by: Demon Transcriber #09079878767653457a3b

Transcript

Fred-8765439-7844*e4: (From here on referred to as "Fred".): It is my job to interview you to determine your damnation status and/or clarification of specifics of your level of damnation in Hell.

John Robert Jonnas: (From here on referred to as "Mr. Jonnas".): Say what you ugly fucker?

(Fred lifts his hand and snaps. Mr. Jonnas' chair disappears, he falls on the floor, leather straps wrap around Mr. Jonnas' wrist and ankles spreading him into Da Vinci's Vitruvian Man.)

Fred: I was hoping today would be easier, I had a rough night last night with the missus, but of course this does give me an opportunity to take out some stress.

(Fred conjures a right sabaton, a medieval knight square-nose boot, then proceeds to put it on.)

Mr. Jonnas: What are you doing?

(Fred starts swinging his foot with the sabaton back and forth.)

Mr. Jonnas: What the fuck are you doing?

(Fred steps in between Mr. Jonnas' legs, begins to take aim at the groin area.)

Mr. Jonnas: Please, don't god please don't.

Fred: Do you know what my wife said? Would you believe that she thinks she is a better ball-buster? I know she is okay at it, but I am good, I mean really good. We have a bet, tonight after I am done classifying your damnation; we are going to have a ball-busting contest. I am going to take some time to practice my technique.

(Mr. Jonnas begins to sob and cry.)

Mr. Jonnas: Please, oh god please.

Fred: If you would mind not flinching, I need to get some good solid hits.

Mr. Jonnas: Please, please don't.

(Fred swings his leg back and kicks Mr. Jonnas in the groin area, slightly off center. Mr. Jonnas' testicles fly up through his abdomen, with one of them flying through the right shoulder area.)

Document 8 Interview: 3445657-ujy5

Fred: Well fuck, shanked that one, this practice is going to take more swings than I thought.

(Fred steps back, waves his hand and heals Mr. Jonnas. Fred then takes aim again and swings for the groin.)

Fred: Fucking slice.

(Fred repeats healing and swinging for the next two days and two hours, improving the entire time.)

Two days and two hours later

Mr. Jonnas: Did…, did…, did I just spit up my ball?

Fred: Yep, that was a great shot. I think I am ready to win the bet with the wife.

(Fred waves at Mr. Jonnas moving him into the chair.)

Fred: Now to continue, it is my job to interview you to determine your damnation status and/or clarification of specifics of your level of damnation in Hell.

(Mr. Jonnas, spits up the other testicle.)

Mr. Jonnas: Okay.

Fred: State your full name.

Mr. Jonnas: John Robert Jonnas

Fred: Mr. Jonnas do you remember the day you died?

Mr. Jonnas: I died?

Fred: Yes, you died, you have been damned, we are here to do some final clarification for your damnation. Now do you remember the day you died?

Mr. Jonnas: I remember some.

Fred: I am sure as we talk it will come back to you. On that day, you had made the decision to burglar a residence.

Mr. Jonnas: Oh yeah, the schoolteacher, I remember him.

Fred: We have some questions about the last day. Can you tell me why you selected him to rob?

Mr. Jonnas: Uh, yeah, I remember, he had a nice car. I don't know what kind, but it was nice, and he was weak looking. I needed an easy one, I was having a run of bad luck.

Fred: What do you mean weak looking?

Mr. Jonnas: He was old and small, and short. Hell, he had a limp. He was an elementary school teacher. All he did was teach little brats. How tough could he be, like I said he was weak.

Fred: Yes, he had a limp, he was missing a foot.

Mr. Jonnas: Wow, really.

Fred: Yes, he was missing a foot. Can you tell me more about that day?

Mr. Jonnas: Yeah sure, I had seen him a few days before at a gas station. He was talking to a woman about her brat; I saw the car and wondered where he got such a nice car. I mean most teachers don't make much money.

Fred: That is correct, did you decide to rob him that day.

Mr. Jonnas: Yeah but I didn't have wheels to follow him, but from the sounds of it he stops by the gas station often.

Fred: You decided to rob him that day but couldn't do it because you did not have a vehicle. Did you acquire a vehicle?

Mr. Jonnas: Yeah, a guy I know OD'd, you know overdosed, so he didn't have a use for his P.O.S.

Fred: P.O.S.?

Mr. Jonnas: Piece of Shit, his hooptie, I mean his car.

Fred: You acquired a car, tell me more about that day.

Mr. Jonnas: Yeah, I got the ride. I headed over to the gas station; I kind of hung out across the road. I couldn't miss his fine car.

Fred: Did he stop at the gas station?

Mr. Jonnas: Nope, but I saw him go by, so I took off after him. I tailed him just like on T.V.

Document 8 Interview: 3445657-ujy5

Fred: You followed him to his house?

Mr. Jonnas: He didn't go home, he went to a cigar place, he was inside for like two hours.

Fred: Yes, he stopped by a cigar lounge. He smoked a cigar and had a glass of whiskey.

Mr. Jonnas: He didn't seem the type, wait they serve whiskey in the cigar place?

Fred: No, but some of the patrons keep bottles there; but that is not important we need to continue with that day.

Mr. Jonnas: He was in there until it got dark, which was ok with me. I couldn't hit his house until dark anyway.

Fred: After he left the cigar lounge, did you follow him to his house?

Mr. Jonnas: Yeah, he stopped by the liquor store and came out with a bottle, but he went straight home after that.

Fred: Was anyone else at his house when he got there?

Mr. Jonnas: Yeah, I think it was his wife and kid, but they left right after he got there. He spent a little while outside talking to his wife before her and the kid left.

Fred: You seem to know exactly what happened, that makes this easy.

Mr. Jonnas: I notice things; I have always been like that.

Fred: That might have failed you in the end. Please continue with your recollection.

Mr. Jonnas: Sure, after the wife and kid left, I was about to go in, but a guy on an old bike showed up. The bike looked like it was old, and it was loud. The teacher hugged the guy when he showed up. I was worried at first, two of them could be an issue. Turned out he was just as old as the teacher.

Fred: The teacher had company, but you were not worried. I take it you proceeded to go in.

Mr. Jonnas: No man, I went around back and looked around first. I looked in the window, saw the teacher and his friend going to a room to the side of the house. Guess he had a "Man Cave" in there. When they went in, I saw it had a bar and TV.

Fred: After you observed them going into the man cave, you decided to break in.

Mr. Jonnas: Yeah, I went around the house but didn't see anything easy. But luck was on my side. I saw an open window on the second floor. I climbed up and in.

Fred: You entered into the house on the second floor. What did you do then?

Mr. Jonnas: I was in a kid's bedroom; I snooped around a little. Saw some good stuff, so I grabbed a pillowcase and started filling it up. I grabbed the game system and games then headed on down the hall. I found the master bedroom, thought I found the jackpot, but the fuckers had a couple of safes, but they were locked.

Fred: I take it you could not open them.

Mr. Jonnas: No way, I went down the hallway and snuck down the stairs. I knew I needed to get the drop on those two guys. I knew I could handle them but didn't want to take chances.

Fred: Sounds reasonable.

Mr. Jonnas: You can't take too many chances breaking into the houses. Bad luck can get you killed.

Fred: Yes, I believe you on that one, what did you do then?

Mr. Jonnas: I went to the kitchen, I saw a knife block, so I grabbed a butcher knife to scare the old men with.

Fred: You were unarmed before this?

Mr. Jonnas: Not really, I had a twenty-five in my pocket, but it's not very intimidating, I figured the knife would scare them.

Fred: I am not sure that was such a good idea.

Mr. Jonnas: Everyone is scared of knives. I know that for sure.

(Fred sat with a stunned look on his face for a full minute.)

Fred: Can you please continue?

Mr. Jonnas: I stashed the pillowcase on the kitchen floor and went looking for some tape. I knew I was gonna need to tape them up. Didn't take me long I found this green tape that looked like duct tape. It should work.

Fred: That is thinking ahead.

Mr. Jonnas: had it under control. I started sneaking back to the man cave. It wasn't very far so I had to be real quiet. I could hear them talking but couldn't make out what they were saying.

Fred: Did you notice anything about the door to the man cave?

Mr. Jonnas: I did, it had something carved in it, it was The Espresso live.

Fred: Are you sure that is what was carved into the door?

Mr. Jonnas: I was thinking the guy must love his expresso.

Fred: It was actually "De Oppresso Liber."

Mr. Jonnas: What is that German or something?

Fred: Latin actually, "De Oppresso Liber" means "To Free the Oppressed."

Document 8 Interview: 3445657-ujy5

Mr. Jonnas: What an odd thing for a teacher to have on his door.

Fred: Yes, for some teachers it would be odd.

Mr. Jonnas: Wait above the door was painted, a green hat, like they wear in those old French movies, with the word "Only" after it.

Fred: You mean a green beret, with the word to the right of it. Maybe meaning Green Berets only?

Mr. Jonnas: I don't know, didn't make much sense to me.

Fred: Continue with your memories.

Mr. Jonnas: The door was cracked, so I crept up and took a look in. I got the scare of my life, they were drinking from the bottle that the teacher bought, but there were three glasses on the table. I was scared I knew I couldn't handle three of them. I thought about leaving but I realized there were only two of them in the room.

Fred: You realized there were only two of them in the room. Did you notice anything else?

Mr. Jonnas: Yeah, they were drinking Johnnie Walker Blue, I have heard that is some good stuff. They had finished half the bottle already. I was thinking it was gonna be easier than I thought, two drunk old men, I knew I could handle them.

Fred: You decided you could handle two very old, very drunk men. Before we go into how that went did you notice anything else about the room.

Mr. Jonnas: Actually, I did, there were a lot of things, I saw two or three swords, a bunch of what looked like certificates on a wall. Oh yeah, the pool table, a really, really nice pool table and the bar where they were sitting.

Fred: Is that all you noticed?

Mr. Jonnas: Yep, I didn't really look around, 'cause I was trying to get close to the old guys.

Fred: Did you get close to them?

Mr. Jonnas: Yeah and you know what the guy that came in on the bike had tears running down his face, the fucker was crying.

Fred: Yes, he was crying, what did you do?

Mr. Jonnas: I let them know I was there and flashed the knife.

Fred: What happened then?

Mr. Jonnas: The teacher looked at the other old guy and said, "don't get blood on the pool table."

Fred: Did they say anything else?

Mr. Jonnas: The guy who rode the bike smiled an evil smile and said, "Fuck yeah, just what I needed."

Afternote:

Mr. Jonnas interrupted the teacher and his friend, who rode the bike, in mourning an old friend who had just died. The teacher, his friend and the one who died were all members of a Team in the United States Army IIth Special Forces Group. He might have realized this if he would have noticed that the Motto carved on the door, or the sword with three lightning bolts across it painted on several items not to mention the Green Beret "Only" above the door. The teacher's friend dispatched Mr. Jonnas violently but not efficiently, he took his time and enjoyed breaking every bone. The teacher and his friend finished the bottle of Johnnie Walker Blue while waiting for the authorities.

Damnation recommendation:

Recommend Mr. Jonnas be assigned as the equipment, the kicking targets, in the ball busting competitions, during the daily demon games. Damnation review in five-hundred years.

Interview: 37869-086-iii5

Demon: Melvin-8762I33-9988*e4

<u>Soul</u>

Given Name: Joseph William Pitt

Also Known as: none

Occupation: Vegan Consultant

Transcribed by: Demon Transcriber #09079878767653457a3b

Transcript

Melvin-8762I33-9988*e4: (From here on referred to as "Melvin".): It is my job to interview you to determine your damnation status and/or clarification of specifics of your level of damnation in Hell.

Joseph William Pitt: (From here on referred to as "Mr. Pitt".): Sure, whatever you say.

Melvin: State your full name.

Mr. Pitt: Joseph William Pitt, age 40, occupation vegan consultant.

Melvin: Vegan consultant?

Mr. Pitt: Yeah, I help people eat better.

Melvin: Were you a vegan?

Mr. Pitt: Yep, I haven't eaten meat since I was I8.

(Melvin reaches a file appears in his hand, he begins to read)

Melvin: You are a liar.

(Melvin waves his hand, and a large blood covered butcher appears.)

Butcher: What can I do for you Sir?

Melvin: Mr. Pitt here says he hasn't eaten meat since he was I8, I want you to slice off meat starting at the souls of his feet, until you have removed the equivalent of the meat Mr. Pitt ate since he was I8.

(Mr. Pitt starts screaming, Melvin waves a hand and a gag with a twelve-inch dildo appears and inserts itself into Mr. Pitts mouth. Leather straps appear around Mr. Pitt in several places completely immobilizing him.)

Butcher: Yes, sir, what size slices?

(A large meat slicer appears. The butcher takes Mr. Pitt and lays him on the pusher part of the meat slicer.)

Melvin: On one please, I like it shaved thin.

Butcher: This could take a while; he had an affinity for lamb, and Big Macs.

Melvin: Do Big Macs contain meat?

Butcher: Not really but we will count it anyway.

Melvin: No worry, we have eternity.

(A butcher counter appears as the slices begin; occasionally a random demon would appear and request some meat. Several times they requested specific cuts from Mr. Pitt.)

Melvin: I was just looking at my notes, turns out Mr. Pitt really liked meat, he has consumed 77088 ounces of meat since he was eighteen. That is double what is normally consumed.

Butcher: Yep, this is gonna take a little while.

Seventy-three days and four hours later

Butcher: 48I8lbs of meat processed from Mr. Pitt.

Melvin: I hope you make a nice bit of profit from that meat.

Butcher: I will make some, but to be honest it was low-grade stuff. Call anytime Sir.

(Butcher waves his hand and the meat slicer, counter, and butcher disappear.)

Melvin: Now that we have taken care of that little issue, we can continue the interview.

(Mr. Pitt laying on the floor, bound and gagged, manages to make a "uhmp" sound.)

Melvin: I almost forgot you must be able to speak.

(Melvin motions to Mr. Pitt, the ball gag disappears, but he is left on the floor.)

Melvin: Mr. Pitt we have some questions about the day you died, do you remember that day.

Mr. Pitt: I ah…I ah…well, I think, I mean.

(Melvin's prehensile tail slides on the floor to Mr. Pitt's ear.)

Melvin: I have found that sometimes the simplest motivation is the best motivation. You, in your life were very proud of your head of hair. It is to you, the best feature you have.

(The prehensile tail sprouts thousands of small arms, with extremely small hands.)

Melvin: I think that we may have to pull each and every hair from your head.

Mr. Pitt: You're going to pull my hair?

(The small hands each grab a single hair, and in a movement similar to the wave at a ballgame rip the hair and skin from Mr. Pitt's head. The effect ends up scalping Mr. Pitt from front to back, Mr. Pitt begins screaming.)

Melvin: Like I said the simplest things are sometimes the best.

(Mr. Pitt screams for several minutes, stops then begins again, stops, then begins crying.)

Melvin: Now that we understand that you need motivation to speak quickly and clearly, I will continue.

Mr. Pitt: I wi…, I wi…, I will be motivated.

Melvin: You were traveling from New Jersey to visit someone in Tucson, Arizona, when you decided to take a detour.

Mr. Pitt: Yeah, I needed to make some quick cash, I figured I would stop in some hick town and hit a bar on a Friday night, and be five states away by Saturday morning.

Melvin: You have done this before?

Mr. Pitt: Yep, whenever I do a trip I always like to hit a bar. I just hide my pistola when I walk in, grab a hostage, get the cash and away I go. Gotta make sure it is near the interstate, so you have an easy getaway.

Melvin: You are familiar with how you think it should go. Where did you decide to hit a bar this time?

Mr. Pitt: I had hit several in Ohio and Pennsylvania, so I decided to hit one in West Virginia, I hadn't hit one there before, but how hard can it be, a bunch of fucking redneck hillbillies.

Melvin: Yes, how hard can it be? Tell me what happened.

Mr. Pitt: I was looking for a big city, but there didn't seem to be any. Lots of bars, but not a lot in big cities. I decided to go further south into

the state. I got lucky there is a place called
Charleston, guess it's the capital or something.

Melvin: Ding, ding you are correct, continue.

Mr. Pitt: There was a place called the "Hillbilly
Heaven" I picked it 'cause I liked the name, and
it was close to the interstate.

Melvin: You have your target, and you have your
way to get away. Seems like you had everything set
up the way you want.

Mr. Pitt: Yep, it looked like a sweet deal. It was
busy, but not too busy.

Melvin: How did you proceed?

Mr. Pitt: Parked my ride near the door, took my
favorite little gun and put it in my pocket, and
went in.

Melvin: What did you find inside Hillbilly Heaven?

Mr. Pitt: I walked in and they had some stupid
country song on. Most everyone was at the bar with
a drink in their hand, with their backs to me.
Nobody even turned to look at me coming into the
place.

Melvin: What did you do?

Mr. Pitt: I made my way to the bar, and ordered a
White Claw, the cute little bartender said they
did not have it, but they had White-dog if I
wanted that. I said "Sure, I will take that," I
mean how different can it be.

Melvin: I take it you did not know what White-dog was.

Mr. Pitt: Nope, I paid my eight dollars, fucking expensive drink. The bartender said she would bring it to my table, I was trying to fit in, so I said, "sure thing." I began walking to a table behind everyone, when the bartender yelled at me, "Hey no smoking ok, we don't need another fire".

Melvin: Was that strange?

Mr. Pitt: Yeah it was, I mean everyone at the bar was smoking something, cigarettes, cigars, and a few pipes too. I really didn't know what she was talking about, but I don't smoke so it really didn't matter.

Melvin: You went to your table, and I assumed you sat down and waited for your drink.

Mr. Pitt: Yep, I was scoping out the place, to see how to get the most money out of it. When a group of bikers walked in, there must have been seven or eight of them. All wearing leather and looking mean. I learned my lessons about bikers a few years ago, so I had decided to delay my plan.

Melvin: Did you get your drink?

Mr. Pitt: Well just after I sat down the bikers showed up. I saw the bartender heading my way with a half glass of water. I was about to say, "I don't need any water," when one of the bikers grabbed it and drank the glass down. His friends started yelling and calling him an asshole and fucking stupid.

Melvin: What did the bartender do?

Mr. Pitt: She kissed him, then she hit him across the jaw. She must have one hell of a punch because he went down hard.

Melvin: Did his friends do anything?

Mr. Pitt: Not really, they just laughed, picked him up and put him on a bench.

Melvin: Did you try to rob the place while the bikers were there?

Mr. Pitt: Hell no, like I said I know better than to try bikers. I waited, the bartender brought me a half glass water, and asked me if I wanted a coke chaser too. I told her I wanted the white dog; she looked at me funny and just said "Okay".

Melvin: Did you get anything else from the bar?

Mr. Pitt: Nope I was just trying to lay low, and if the bartender thought she was gonna rip me off by ignoring my order I had something for her. Just had to wait for the proper time.

Melvin: Did that time come?

Mr. Pitt: Yeah, the bikers finally left, but the guy who had grabbed my water stayed, he must have drunk a lot while he was there because he passed out. I heard the loud bikes ride away.

Melvin: You sat there waiting the entire time, drinking water, waiting?

Mr. Pitt: I didn't even touch the water, I was just watching and listening to the horrible music.

Melvin: When did you decide to make your move?

Mr. Pitt: It was getting late, and a few of the customers had left. The bar was full, but I didn't expect any of the regular drunks to leave. I dumped my water on the floor, and waved at the bartender, pointing to my glass.

Melvin: Did she respond?

Mr. Pitt: Yeah, she saw me pointing at the glass. She looked a little shocked, guess she didn't want to give me another glass of water, but she shrugged and shook her head yes. All I had to do was wait for her to bring the water over, grab her with my trusty little pistola, and force everyone else to give me their money and grab the cash from the register. After that it's just out the door and away I go.

Melvin: That was your plan, seems straight forward enough.

Mr. Pitt: You would think it would be easy, when the bartender came over, with another half glass of water, she asked for eight dollars for the drink. Hell, I never even had the first drink; she wanted me to pay for a second for her not to bring it to me.

Melvin: Now that does not seem fair.

Mr. Pitt: That's when I grabbed her, but she was seriously strong too, it took everything I had to get her and get my pistola on her head.

Melvin: How did the patrons react?

Mr. Pitt: I moved her toward the bar, she yelled at someone named Junior to get his attention.

Melvin: Did she get this Junior's attention?

Mr. Pitt: Yeah, this short shit turned around. Took one look at her, then me, then my pistola and laughed. I have no idea what he was laughing about, but he was just cracking up.

Melvin: He found the situation funny?

Mr. Pitt: Maybe, I was thinking he was a little wrong in the head, that is when the rest of the bar patrons turned around.

Melvin: Did they react the same way?

Mr. Pitt: Fuckers, they all laughed!

Melvin: So just to get this clear, everyone in the bar laughed at you?

Mr. Pitt: Fuck yeah, I mean I had my pistola to the head of this bitch, and they are laughing at me.

Melvin: You keep saying pistola, what kind of gun was it?

Mr. Pitt: It's a cool little cobra derringer.

(Melvin just stares blankly at Mr. Pitt.)

Melvin: What caliber is it?

Mr. Pitt: What do you mean?

Melvin: What kind of bullets does it shoot?

Mr. Pitt: Rifle bullets, that's why I bought it.

Melvin: Do you mean twenty-two long rifle?

Mr. Pitt: Yep, that's the one.

Melvin: Let me make sure I am getting this correct. The situation is you are in a bar, in Charleston, West Virginia, holding the bartender hostage with a 2-shot derringer that shoots .22 long-rifle.

(Mr. Pitt stares at Melvin with a confused look on his face.)

Mr. Pitt: Yeah, that's it.

Melvin: I think I know why they were laughing.

Mr. Pitt: They were laughing at me, but I had the gun. I had the gun pointed at the bitch.

Melvin: Yet they laughed at you, what happened next.

Mr. Pitt: I didn't know what to do, I was getting scared, so I released the bartender, and took a step back. I remember stepping in something wet, it must have been my water I dumped out.

Melvin: Yes, it was what you dumped out.

Mr. Pitt: I was just standing there looking at the patrons; they were laughing. I really didn't know what to do.

Melvin: What broke this ah…laughing standoff?

Mr. Pitt: The bartender, she hit me. Now I know why the biker went down so fast, she was wearing brass knuckles. She hit me with brass knuckles.

Melvin: That would explain the quick dropping of the biker.

Mr. Pitt: I went down hard. I didn't get knocked out, completely I remember landing in something wet. Funny it smelled like alcohol.

Melvin: There may be a reason for that.

Mr. Pitt: I saw that guy, Junior, walk over, he was smoking a cigar…I remember rolling over, I was covered in something wet. Junior was just standing there looking at his cigar and then me then back to his cigar. I don't know what he was thinking. Then he held up the cigar, looked at it, and dropped it.

Melvin: Do you have any memories after that?

Mr. Pitt: Pain, lots of pain, all over my back, and my head, a burning pain.

Melvin: Is that the last thing you remember?

Mr. Pitt: No, I remember riding in the back of a truck. I remember thinking how it felt like we were going up and up and up.

Melvin: Please Continue.

Mr. Pitt: I remember some type of gate, then a hole, falling, and dark. I mean real dark, dark like I have never seen. I couldn't see any lights or stars. Nothing.

Afternotes:

Mr. Pitt deserves extra damnation for wasting a glass of very flammable White Dog, the local moonshine. Mr. Pitt did not die that night, he died two days later at the bottom of a condemned coal mine.

Damnation Recommendation:

Recommend Mr. Pitt spends his damnation in his body in the mine. Damnation review in twelve-hundred-fifty years.

DOCUMENT 10

INTERVIEW: 378696556786-I5

Interview: 378696556786-i5

Demon: Chad-III00022876-986*e4

Soul

Given Name: Kenneth Longfellow Smith

Also Known as: Smitty

Occupation: Functioning Alcoholic Soldier

Translator: Sargon of Akkad, also known as Sargon the Great of Mesopotamian

Transcribed by: Demon Transcriber #09079878767653457a3b

Transcript

Chad-III00022876-986*e4: (From here on referred to as "Chad".): It is my job to interview you to determine your damnation status and/or clarification of specifics of your level of damnation in Hell.

Kenneth Longfellow Smith: (From here on referred to as "Mr. Smith".): Could you say that again?

(Chad pauses and stares at Mr. Smith)

Chad: It is my job to interview you to determine your damnation status and/or clarification of specifics of your level of damnation in Hell. Can you state your full name?

(Mr. Smith sits up straighter and his composure changes into a more formal sitting position.)

Mr. Smith: Kenneth Longfellow Smith, Sir that sounds very formal, am I in trouble?

Chad: You could say that, we are just here to work out the details of your damnation.

(Mr. Smith loses all formality and looks extremely stressed.)

Mr. Smith: Fuck, fuck, fuck, god damn motherfucking twatwaffles, those broke dick boxes of rocks numb nut motherfucking oxygen thieving jar heads. I am never gonna make formation now.

Chad: Mr. Smith is there an issue?

Mr. Smith: Ficken leatherneck, busu fucking, cherryboy hero wanna be like me pendeja.

(Chad waves at Mr. Smith and a ball gage and straps appear, Mr. Smith still tries to speak but the mumbles are all that can be heard.)

Chad: Although I appreciate your ability to cuss in several languages you called them pendeja, not pendejo. They were males so pendejo is correct.

(Mr. Smith starts shaking his head back and forth sideways, Chad waves and the ball gage disappears.)

Mr. Smith: Not if I get my hands on those amzi jarheads I will make them a pendeja. I will rip their fucking nuts off.

Chad: I am not familiar with "amzi."

Mr. Smith: It's an acronym A, M, Z, I it stands for all muscle zero intelligence.

Chad: Got it, but we need to get back to the interview.

Mr. Smith: Well hell, I guess I am fucked so might as well go along, got any Copenhagen?

(Chad stops canting his head sideways and just shakes his head side to side.)

Chad: We are here to determine some details about the day you died, which means that I don't think you have to worry about missing that formation.

Mr. Smith: Well hero ranger, there is some good fucking news.

(Chad pauses for a minute.)

Chad: You are in Hell. Do you realize that?

Mr. Smith: Can't be, I didn't sign into my old unit, that place was in bum fuck Egypt. I got the Big Green Dick every damn week, layouts every goddamn four day. Nothing but new L-fucking-Ts, and the duty roster changed hourly. Not to mention Desert Queens every fucking where, all wanting to be dependapotamus. Not one decent cockpit in the AO. I was a cunt hair from being on the carpet every wakeup. It was nothing but REMFs and PT rats.

Chad: I didn't understand anything you just said.

(Chad conjures a ball gage on Mr. Smith and some
paperwork. He studies the paperwork for a minute,
then picks up a phone that appears when he reaches
for it.)

Chad: Send me Sargon of Akkad. Yes, the
Mesopotamian.

(Chad hangs up the phone, and a Man standing
akimbo in generic battle fatigues appears, with a
close crop beard. He is wearing a sidearm on his
hip. Carrying a medium length spear with two rings
on it.)

Chad: This Sargon of Akkad, you may know him as
Sargon the Great of Mesopotamian, he will be
assisting me in this interview as a translator and
facilitator.

Sargon of Akkad (From here on referred to as
"Sargon".): Well we have another ground pounder,
don't worry I will un-fuck this clusterfuck. Chad,
what did you need me to translate?

Chad: I asked him if he realized he was in hell.
This was his response.

(Chad waves his hand. Mr. Smith's voice begins to
speak from the air.)

Mr. Smith's voice: Can't be, I didn't sign into my
old unit, that place was in bum fuck Egypt. I got
the Big Green Dick every damn week, layouts every
goddamn four day. Nothing but new L-fucking-Ts,
and the duty roster changed hourly. Not to mention

Desert Queens every fucking where, all wanting to be dependapotamus. Not one decent cockpit in the AO. I was a cunt hair from being on the carpet every wakeup. It was nothing but REMFs and PT rats.

Sargon: Got it, loosely translated, he disagrees with you about this being Hell. He says he is not assigned to his prior unit which he considers hell, that it was in the middle of nowhere. That the old unit used to fail him consistently every week. He continues, that every chance they had to have four consecutive days off over the weekend the unit required them to lay out equipment and inventory it. All the officers were of the lieutenant variety, very low ranking and inexperienced. The duty roster which he had to follow, and had to plan around, were not consistent and changed regularly without warning. He also points out that the place was full of extremely ugly women who only had men interested during deployments when other more attractive women are not available. He also explains the women that were available are not interested in anything except depending on him for his benefits and pay. As a re-enforcement he points out that good looking women who are willing to engage in sexual congress, the "cockpit," are not in the area of operation. He points out that every day, he was always on the verge of going to see the commander for non-judicial punishment. The worst part is that it was full of soldiers that normally worked the rear echelons and/or spent all the time doing physical exercise.

Chad: He said that? Do you need any time with him before we begin?

Sargon: Yeah, I need a minute, can you undo the restraints.

(Chad gestures, and the restraints on Mr. Smith disappeared.)

Mr. Smith: Man, you look like you taught Jesus to march time.

(Sargon turns to Mr. Smith, puts his hands on the table.)

Sargon: Listen here you poor excuse for a shit sandwich. I was doing drills when the Big J wasn't even a twinkle in his daddy's sky. I was stacking bodies, before the first queen of England was blowing the king on his throne. I did my first deployment long before Marc Anthony Jodied Julius Caesar with Cleopatra. If you think you can give me any shit, I will smoke you faster than a ring knocker talks about west point. You just take those dick beaters and plant your sorry ass in that chair until you are told to un-ass it. Do you read me?

Mr. Smith: Lima Charlie, Sir.

(Mr. Smith quickly moves to the chair and sits in a modified attention position.)

Document I0 Interview: 378696556786-i5

Sargon: Chad, he is ready and willing to cooperate.

Chad: Thank you for the assistance, I would request you stay.

Sargon: No problem Chad.

Chad: Now we can continue with the interview. Mr. Smith in reference to your last day. I would like some details. Do you remember that day?

(Mr. Smith looks at Sargon who nods.)

Mr. Smith: Affirmative.

Chad: Towards the end of your workday, you and several of your buddies decided to go out. Can you begin there?

Mr. Smith: Sir, what kind of details would you like?

Chad: Just tell me about it, feel free to elaborate on whatever details you think are important.

(Mr. Smith looked at Sargon and shrugged.)

Sargon: Chad says you're fucked anyways so you might as well just tell him the truth.

Mr. Smith: Oh, I am used to that.

Chad: That is not what I said.

Sargon: But that is what you meant, as far as he is concerned.

Chad: Oh. Mr. Smith tell me about your day.

Mr. Smith: It was a Friday afternoon we were busting our hump to get done 'cause it was getting close to beer thirty. I filled up the hummer but got on the shitlist for calling a donkey dick a Donkey Dick.

Chad: Uh?

Sargon: They were working hard because it was Friday and he was ready to drink a beer. He filled the military vehicle up with fuel, but his supervisor was upset with him for calling the fuel nozzle for the five-gallon fuel can the derogatory name "Donkey Dick".

Chad: Your supervisor was upset with you, is that why you decided to go out that night?

Mr. Smith: Sergeant Notso is always a prick, we decided to go out that night because we had a FNG and my bro turned into a two-digit-midget.

Chad: Wait, your paperwork says your Sergeants name was Bright?

Sargon: Notso is an insult, as in not so bright, not so intelligent, et cetera. Before you ask a FNG is a fucking new guy. A two-digit-Midget is someone who is leaving in less than a hundred days, ninety-nine days or less.

Chad: Okay, so you and your friends decided to go out. Tell me about that.

Mr. Smith: Sure, so Smitty, the FNG, and myself…

Chad: Wait I thought you were "Smitty?"

Mr. Smith: There are always a few Smittys, his last name was Smith too, no relation. So Smitty two, the FNG and myself, decided to preload before we went out. It was a special occasion, Smitty two had a combat bottle of Soju that his ex-juicy girl wife brought over for him.

(Mr. Smith looks at Sargon and waits.)

Sargon: He says that the three of them decided to drink before they went out to save money on the bar tab. His friend who is also named Smith, has an ex-wife who was a "Juicy Girl" who was a prostitute in South Korea. They are known for asking for expensive drinks, which are nothing but juice, per the name "Juicy Girl". The ex-wife had at some time given the other Smith an extremely large bottle of Soju, the alcohol well known in South Korea for getting soldiers in trouble.

Chad: Got it.

Mr. Smith: There we were, preloading when a couple of Redlegs started banging on the door. Turns out the FNG went to basic with one of them.

Chad: Redlegs?

Sargon: Soldiers with a Field Artillery MOS.

Mr. Smith: Now we had myself, Smitty two, the FNG, three RedLegs, and an empty bottle of Soju.

Somehow, we picked up a supply bitch, but it's cool 'cause he was the one with a POV.

Chad: Wait, the paperwork did not say anything about a female with you. Where did she come from.

Sargon: The "Supply bitch" is a male soldier, and a POV is a personally owned vehicle, the supply soldier had a car.

Chad: Ah…. Okay.

(Mr. Smith is getting excited, almost bouncing in his seat.)

Mr. Smith: No shit there we were cruising, but we didn't know where the fuck to go. But it turns out that one of the Redlegs knew about a place that navy wives stepout, that's an idea I could get behind.

Sargon: Stepout means they navy wives are looking for extramarital sex, usually when their husbands are out to sea.

Mr. Smith: Must suck to be in the navy. The supply bitch was sober and got real pissed at the rest of us for fucking up his car. As soon as we hit the bar, he fucking popped smoke. What a fucking Blue Falcon.

Chad: Popped smoke, blue falcon?

Sargon: The supply soldier left quickly and he became a Blue Falcon because "fucked" them by leaving them there. Blue Falcons are soldiers that

sabotage other soldiers because of their lack of
loyalty and integrity.

Mr. Smith: Yeah that buddy fucker, but it turned
out cool cause it was happy hour, it was one
dollar shots all around.

Chad: You continued drinking, when did the night
start to go wrong?

Mr. Smith: It was all good, some serious split
tail showed up. With only six guys in the bar
things were looking good, then we got a bag of
dicks. The goddamn Uncle Sam's misguided children
show up. A whole goddamn company walked in the
door.

Chad: Split tail, bag of dicks and children in the
bar?

Sargon: Split tail is females, bag of dicks is a
really bad situation, and Uncle Sam's misguided
children is U.S.M.C, United States Marine Corp,
not children.

Mr. Smith: If that isn't bad enough the damn FNG
decides to get in a big dick contest with what
looks to be an FNG with the fucking Marines.

Sargon: Fucking Cherrys!

Chad: Cherrys?

Sargon: New guys, that have not had their hymen
busted by experience.

Mr. Smith: Yeah fucking Cherrys, but Smitty two calmed things down, then one of the of the Redlegs disappears. His friends said he talked a barracks bunny into a freedom blowjob.

Chad: Barracks bunny, freedom blowjob?

Sargon: A female that is trying to get with a military guy, hangs around barracks and the places military men frequent, and freedom blowjob is fellatio preformed right before or after a military member deploys in honor of the freedom they are defending.

Chad: Is that when the issues happened?

Chad: What did you do?

Mr. Smith: I decided to cool things down a little, jokes always help.

Chad: You told jokes?

Mr. Smith: Yep, I stood up on a table and told my second favorite Marine joke. What does a submarine and a Marine have in common? They are both full of semen.

Sargon: You Dip Shit.

Chad: What happened then?

Mr. Smith: Nothing, everyone stopped and looked. Then I told my favorite Marine joke. How do you kill a marine? Throw sand against a brick wall and tell them to hit the beach.

Sargon: You stupid fucking ground pounder.

Chad: Did something happen then?

Mr. Smith: Well yeah, every fucking thing happened then. All hell broke loose, assholes and elbows everywhere. I punched, kicked and bit anything I could get my hands one. Still got my bell rang, but I stayed up.

Chad: Do you remember anything else?

Mr. Smith: Some pud-puller called the goddamn police? I screamed for Smitty two, and told him to didi mao. It didn't take a genius to see what was coming our way.

Chad: Didi Mao?

Sargon: "Didi Mao" basically means get moving fast.

Chad: Did you leave with your friends?

Mr. Smith: I wish, they were on the other side of the bar, I headed for a door that said kitchen, I figured I could head out the back.

Chad: Did you escape the bar?

Mr. Smith: Yeah, but several jarheads came out with me but we all headed in different ways. I took off running; I really didn't need any more issues than I already had. I was drunk as hell, but I have run drunk more than once in my life.

Chad: Did you get caught by the police?

Document IO Interview: 378696556786-15

Mr. Smith: I E and E'd my ass off, found some houses and started running through alleys and yards.

Chad: E and E'd?

Sargon: Escape and evaded, he got away and hid from the police.

Chad: You were running through the alleys and yards. How did that proceed?

Mr. Smith: That is where it gets fuzzy. I found a side street, I was about to cross it when I saw a house with a fence, with a pool full of women. I knew it was stupid, but I struck a conversation up with a hottie. I figured if I could get in with them, I would be safe with them for a while.

Chad: You started talking to one of them?

Mr. Smith: Yeah, there were a few guys, but the odds were in my favor, looked to be 6 or 7 extra females there. Hell, I might get lucky. I decided to invite myself in, and no shit, one told me sure come on in, that there was a gate around the side, and it was unlocked.

Chad: Did you go through the gate?

Mr. Smith: I thought it would be cooler just to jump the fence, but that didn't go so well.

Chad: What happened?

Mr. Smith: I made it up the outside just fine, but I guess I was drunker than I thought.

Chad: Why is that?

Mr. Smith: Do you know what a lawn gnome garden is?

Chad: A place in a yard where people set up a little village of lawn gnomes, the little statues with pointy hats.

Mr. Smith: Yeah, I always thought they were a little stupid.

Chad: What does this have to do with getting over the fence?

Mr. Smith: Well, like I said I was drunker than I thought. I scaled the outside just fine, but when I went to jump down on the inside, I slipped.

Chad: You fell on the inside.

Mr. Smith: Yeah face first into about 40 or 50 lawn gnomes, with those pointy hats.

Damnation recommendation:

After speaking to Sargon and him explaining that Mr. Smith was not cavalry, he recommended Mr. Smith work as the barback at Fiddlers Green, located halfway down the trail to Hell. Alcohol will not be able to work on Mr. Smith, and he will have his genitals removed to restrict any type sexual enjoyment. Recommend review in five-hundred years.

Damnation adjustment:

Mr. Smith is not allowed nicotine of any kind.

Damnation adjustment:

Mr. Smith is now restricted from fighting with the cavalry.

Damnation adjustment:

Mr. Smith is now restricted from talking about weapons.

Damnation adjustment:

Mr. Smith is not allowed to play any card games, especially spades.

Damnation adjustment:

Mr. Smith is not allowed to play dominoes of any kind.

Damnation adjustment:

Mr. Smith is not allowed to quote movies.

Damnation adjustment:

Mr. Smith is not allowed to touch paracord.

Damnation adjustment:

Mr. Smith is not allowed to workout, run, or go into "P.T. mode".

Damnation adjustment:

Mr. Smith now is unable to talk about anything
military, he must listen to every story told, and
must respond with "If you ain't Cav you ain't
shit."

DOCUMENT 11

INTERVIEW: 347980-2-UJPI5

Interview: 347980-2-ujpi5

Demon: Ned-098683-976*e4

Soul

Given Name: Dale Allen Ponce

Also Known as: none

Occupation: Scam Artist, Thief

Transcribed by: Demon Transcriber #0907987876765-3457a3b

Transcript

Ned-098683-976*e4: (From here on referred to as "Ned".): It is my job to interview you to determine your damnation status and/or clarification of specifics of your level of damnation in Hell.

Dale Allen Ponce: (From here on referred to as "Mr. Ponce".): Damnation, you mean like in Hell?

Ned: Got it on the first try, but not like in Hell, you are in Hell.

Mr. Ponce: Oh lord Jesus…

(Ned reaches out and stuffs his hand in Mr. Ponces' mouth, ripping the cheeks and jaw when he does.)

Ned: Maybe you do not understand, it is too late for that. Now as I said we are here to clarify some specifics on your damnation. We have the bulk of the information we are mainly concerned with the day you died. Do you remember your last day on earth?

(Ned removes his hand from the mouth, the mouth heals enough to speak, but not completely.)

Mr. Ponce: I think I recall, it's a little fuzzy but I think I can answer the questions.

Ned: Good, I want to make this quick. I have a golf tournament I want to play in.

(Mr. Ponce visibly brightens and begins smiling.)

Mr. Ponce: I was pretty good at golf so maybe I can help.

(Ned slants his head sideways, looking hard at Mr. Ponce.)

Ned: I think you can help, I might as well practice while I can.

(Ned waves his hand, Mr. Ponce slams to the floor, straps appear restricting the arms to the torso and the legs together.)

Mr. Ponce: I can't help you strapped like this!

Ned: Oh, but you can. I have not had enough time to practice my drives lately. I also need practice on my chip shots. You will be of great help.

(Ned gestures and a wooden driver appears in his hands, along with a glove and golf shoes. He walks over to where Mr. Ponce is strapped to the floor.

When he does Mr. Ponce's pants rip open exposing his genitals. Ned positions himself to where the driver is located just at the groin area.)

Mr. Ponce: Please no god no please god no I will do anything…please anything.

Ned: It is not nice to make noise when someone is trying to hit the ball, you should be quiet during golf!

(Ned reaches down, and rips Mr. Ponces' tongue out of his mouth, gestures and a golf tee gently lifts one of Mr. Ponces' testicles up to just over his thighs. Ned takes aim.)

Ned: Four!

(Ned fully swings the driver the testicle makes a slight curve to the right. Mr. Ponce moans in pain.)

Ned: Sliced it, well I have plenty of time.

(Another tee lifts Mr. Ponce's other testicle to the ready to hit position. Ned fully swings the driver. The testicle also curves slightly to the right.)

Ned: This could take some time, but I have all day.

(Mr. Ponce's testicles return to the starting position, Ned positions to the ready to swing position. Mr. Ponce has tears running down his face.)

Ned: Man, I love this game just you and the balls.

(Ned practices his drives for the next six hours, slightly improving every swing until his slice is miniscule.)

Ned: See I knew you could help.

(Mr. Ponce moves his head in a nod and tries to smile.)

Ned: Now onto the chipping.

(The driver is replaced in Ned's hands with a chipping wedge. The tee disappears leaving the testicles lying close to Mr. Ponce's general groin area. Ned lines up and swings, hitting the ball and removing a portion of Mr. Ponce's groin area. Ned kicks it back into place, and the testicles return to the body.)

Ned: I always get too deep when I pitch and chip. I guess I need to practice more than I thought.

(Ned continues to practice for seven hours, never really improving.)

Ned: I guess that will have to do, thank you for your help, not everyone volunteers to be sports equipment.

(Ned waves away is club, glove and shoes returning to normal office attire, Mr. Ponce is released and is lifted to the chair returning to his seated position.)

Mr. Ponce: What in God's name was that?

Ned: You are mistaken, not in God's name, in Satan's name.

Mr: Ponce: Why? I didn't do anything that bad, I may have told a lie or two.

Ned: Mr. Ponce, you did more than tell a lie or two. You swindled and stole from…

(Ned grasps in the air and a file appears, he consults it.)

Ned: …From no less than five grandmothers, twelve unwed mothers, one of which you were sleeping with, wait no, that was one of the grandmothers. Thirty-five fathers that were just making ends meet for their families, six honest businessmen…

(Ned looks up surprised.)

Ned: Where did you find the honest businessman? Filed and got government money that was destined for the needy, short changed 42 female prostitutes, 6 male prostitutes…

Mr. Ponce: Wait, they were all women.

Ned: You did not look, closely did you? But to continue, six different charities, stole money out of a blind musician's guitar case, and swindled two politicians, wait the swindling the two politicians went to the "good".

Mr. Ponce: You cannot know all of that!

Ned: We do and that is just the stuff highlighted, I can go down the entire list, including the number of times you autoerotic asphyxiated and masturbated with your club the Bronies.

Mr. Ponce: Oh.

Ned: We know all about you. We just want a little more information about the day you died.

Mr. Ponce: Well I don't think I am going to cooperate. I will just sit here and say nothing.

Ned: Mr. Ponce, we in Hell have tried to modernize and keep up with the modern world, but some souls insist upon being difficult. In the spirit of trying to get you to cooperate, I think a short stay in one of the old standard damnation areas will do you some good. Say hello to Charles Ponzi from Ned-098683-976*e4, while you spend a short fifty years in the eighth circle of Dante Alighieri's Hell.

(A portal opens and sucks Mr. Ponce into the damnation area based on the eighth circle of Dante Alighieri's Inferno.)

Interview stops for 50 years

(A ceiling portal opens and drops Mr. Ponce to his chair. He is covered in mud from the waist up, and his feet are burned off.)

Ned: Welcome back Mr. Ponce, I hoped that short stay helped you see why we are trying to modernize.

Mr. Ponce: I was…I was…I was head down in mud, the entire time…and my feet were burnt…Why?

Ned: Exactly my point, you had no idea what your damnation was for. Incidentally, it was because your worst sin was being a simoniac, which means you used a position you had to get money from someone selling favors or that should belong to God. Your feet were burned in accordance, proportional to your guilt. Very 14th century if you ask me.

Mr. Ponce: I guess that makes sense, I kind of see the logic.

Ned: Good, now about the last day you died, have you decided to cooperate?

Mr. Ponce: Yes, God yes.

Ned: What do you remember about that day?

Mr. Ponce: … I remember, I remember, oh yeah, the dork.

Ned: The dork?

Mr. Ponce: That is just what I called him in my head, Derrick, he was a computer programmer. He made a bunch of money with some stupid apps he wrote. He wasn't super rich, but he could afford all these toys, drones and such.

Ned: Were you trying to swindle him?

Mr. Ponce: I was running a nice little scam where I sold him some property, he wanted to build some kind of geek place. You know where they can dress up and play their stupid games.

Ned: It was the property the county had wanted a golf course to be built on.

Mr. Ponce: Yeah, it would have been a perfect golf course too, just close enough to the city not to be a long drive, but far enough out to be out of the city.

Ned: Why did the golf course get canceled?

Mr. Ponce: The little shit had enough money to pull support from it.

Ned: Is that what made you decide to go after him?

Mr. Ponce: Hell yeah, he got the golf course canceled, not to mention he must have had a ton of money, I bet he was worth at least a million.

Ned: Thirty-two million actually.

Mr. Ponce: What? Thirty-two million, and he lived in that little four-bedroom house.

Ned: Yes, he liked the area.

Mr. Ponce: He liked the area? He didn't even have a car. He took an Uber everywhere.

Ned: Tell me about the last day of your life.

Mr. Ponce: It was all good, until about 3 o'clock, I found out that Derrick had used a small drone to film our meetings. He had avoided sending money but that is not unusual. The little fuck must have known something was up if he was filming the meetings.

Ned: What was the swindle?

Mr. Ponce: I was selling him the piece of property at a little elevated price, I25% of what it was worth.

Ned: If he is willing to pay it how is that a swindle?

Mr. Ponce: I didn't really own the property.

Ned: If you wanted to make money, why didn't you lower the price?

Mr. Ponce: Nothing runs off money like being too cheap. He thought I was just gouging him because I knew the county wanted a golf course there.

Ned: What is the big deal with the drones?

Mr. Ponce: They had my face, so they would have found out my real name with a little digging. Not to mention if they caught me on video, it was proof.

Ned: You were not using your name. What name were you using?

Mr. Ponce: The gracious Pastor William Bailey, Bill to his friends.

Ned: You were impersonating a member of a church, and he believed you were selling your own property?

Mr. Ponce: Yes, but he believed the church was selling the property and that I was just a go between.

Ned: I understand the basics, he believed you were representing a church, and that you were charging so much because the county wanted a golf course there.

Mr. Ponce: Correct, I try to keep things simple. But he was delaying sending the money, and I was getting worried. I had a friend of mine check out Derrick, just basic stuff but they found out about the drone. Actually, my friend was recording a meeting with Derrick using a drone and just happened to record Derricks drone by mistake.

Ned: You found out that you were being recorded; did you confront Derrick?

Mr. Ponce: Yeah, outside of a little taco place he goes to every Tuesday. You know what that little fuck told me, that he recorded all of his meetings, he said "it was perfectly legal" That explains why he always wanted to meet outside.

Ned: Did he say anything else?

Mr. Ponce: Yeah, he said I was a "Small Minded..." I don't remember the word, but it sounded bad.

Ned: "Small minded imbecile" was the phrase he used.

Mr. Ponce: After he got in the Uber, I jumped in my car and raced to his house. I knew where he lived from my research. I figured I would just break in real quick before he got home and grab the hard drive with the video on it.

Ned: You do not keep up with technology do you, never mind rhetorical question. Did you break in?

Mr. Ponce: Yeah, I zoomed past him to get to his house, the Ubers always take too long. So, I figured I had a little time to figure it out. I pulled around the back of his three-car garage, why did he even have a garage, no car let alone three, must have come with the house.

Ned: I am sure you are correct.

Mr. Ponce: As I was saying I pulled around to behind his garage to hide my car and figured I would kick in the back door or something. I didn't want to have to come back at night, that always seems so low class to break into a house at night.

Ned: Did the break in go smoothly?

Mr. Ponce: Not really, I thought it was an old house, and would just take a few kicks to get in. He must have had the door reinforced because I couldn't get it to budge. I tried the windows but that didn't work either.

Ned: Did you get in?

Mr. Ponce: I saw an open window on the second floor, it looked like I could get in, but I couldn't reach. Would you believe I had to pull my car around and climb on the roof, I think I put a dent in my Mercedes.

Ned: Yes, you did, a pretty severe one in fact.

Mr. Ponce: Well shit, and not a repair place in a hundred miles.

Ned: I do not believe you are going to have to worry about the car. Can you continue please?

Mr. Ponce: Oh yeah. I used my car to reach the second-floor window, it was to the bathroom. I twisted my knee going in, but I got it. It was small, I mean really small just a shower. How can people live like that? I have closets bigger than that bathroom.

Ned: Had, not have, now go on.

Mr. Ponce: I figured I needed to find his office so I could grab what I wanted. I started searching, it was weird. Derrick had all kinds of odd stuff in each room.

Ned: What kind of odd stuff?

Mr. Ponce: One room was full of Star Wars crap. I mean not the new stuff but like from the 70s. It was wall to wall geek crap. Another was a bedroom, but it was decorated in something called Firefly, I don't know what that is. The third bedroom must have been his, it had clothes, a bed and an odd assortment of just everything. Remember the robot from the Rocky movie that Paulie had, he had one of those, but it was turned off.

Ned: What about the fourth bedroom?

Mr. Ponce: I waited until last to go in there. The door said dungeon, I was expecting some type of sex playroom. But all it had in it, was a big round table with chairs. It also had two fridges, one full of Dr. Pepper, and the other full of junk food. There were fantasy posters on three of the walls, and a white board on the other…Meeting room maybe?

Ned: Did you notice anything else? Anything unusual?

Mr. Ponce: I remember hearing a buzzing sound, it was just there, not like a bee, but buzzing.

Ned: That is all you noticed?

Mr. Ponce: Yeah nothing else, I continued down the stairs. I went down there, and all I found was a kitchen, and what I guess was his home entertainment center. He had a big room, with a TV that took up the entire wall. Theater seating, and surround sound and I guess game systems. He also had what looked like a racecar chair on wheels. But no office.

Ned: What about the buzzing?

Mr. Ponce: It was still there, like it was following me. I looked for the source but couldn't find it. To be honest it was kind of messing with my head.

Ned: What did you do then?

Mr. Ponce: I searched the house again, I didn't even find a laptop, I was getting worried, I knew he had the stuff, did he have an office somewhere else. I was about to call in some help when it hit me. The three-car garage, he didn't have a car so that must be the place. I almost ran to the garage.

Ned: How did you get in the garage?

Mr. Ponce: Now that you mention it, that is what was odd, it had a really nice electronic lock on it that beeped when I walked up to it. When I tried the door, it was unlocked.

Ned: What about the buzzing?

Mr. Ponce: Hold on, I don't think it followed me in.

Ned: What happened once you got into the garage?

Mr. Ponce: It was dark, I guess the garage door windows were covered, and it was cold. Outside it was like 90, but the garage must have been air conditioned because it was cool. I started reaching for the light switch. That's when I got the surprise of my life the door behind me shut, as soon as it did the lights came on.

Ned: What did you see?

Mr. Ponce: Robots, lots of robots, and robot parts, and computers. It looked like some futuristic lab.

Ned: Was anything moving?

Mr. Ponce: Some of the completed robots turned their heads to look at me. Some of them turned their bodies.

Ned: What did you do?

Mr. Ponce: I turned to run away, but the door was locked, I tried kicking it and hurt my knee even more. I don't think I could have knocked it down anyway it felt solid.

Ned: After you found the door locked what did you do?

Mr. Ponce: I moved along the wall where I thought I would find the garage doors. Turns out the doors had been removed and solid steel doors installed. They looked like a goddamn safe door. I was starting to get scared.

Ned: Did you try anything else?

Mr. Ponce: Yeah, I tried smashing the electronic lock that was on the door where I came in, I barely put a scratch on it. I was getting really scared now. I knew I didn't have much time before Derrick came home. Then I remembered what I was looking for in the first place. The videos, they must be there somewhere. I started looking around, that is when I tried my phone; I could call someone to open the door from the outside.

Ned: Did you get a hold of anyone?

Mr. Ponce: No, I didn't have any signal at all.

Ned: What about the videos? Did you find them?

Mr. Ponce: I didn't find anything, nothing they could be on. That is when I decided that I needed to smash the computer, he must have the videos on there.

Ned: That could be an assumption, not one I would make. Did you smash the computer?

Mr. Ponce: I tried, but there wasn't anything but some chairs to hit it with.

Ned: Is that what you did?

Mr. Ponce: Oh yeah, I hit it as hard as I could, I got some sparks, I must have done some damage. But I slipped, my knee failed me, and I went down hard. I think I broke my arm when I did, not to mention my ribs hurt like a mother fucker too.

Ned: You were helpless on the floor. Laying there with the computer smashed, what did you think was going to happen.

Mr. Ponce: I was expecting Derrick to come home, I might spend some time dealing with the misdemeanor, but it would be better than the other charges.

Ned: Did Derrick show up?

Mr. Ponce: Nope, I laid there for a while, waiting, nothing. Then the funniest thing happened, there was all this glass broken on the floor. You know those things that sweep the floor, little round robots?

Ned: The Roomba.

Mr. Ponce: Yeah, the rumbi, roombi, rambi… Whatever, so there are like four or five that come out and start sweeping up the glass. After about an hour, there is not a piece of glass on the floor just me, in all my pain.

Ned: You are there, but you are not dead. Did Derrick come home?

Mr. Ponce: No, but I had another visitor?

Ned: Who visited you?

Mr. Ponce: Not a "who" but a "what," a small little mouse, came and started going all around me. I tried to shoo it away, but no luck and I couldn't move. I just laid there.

Ned: Did anything else happen?

Mr. Ponce: Yeah, I heard a song, but it was not loud, just like coming out of super small speakers. It took me a minute to figure it out.

Ned: What song?

Mr. Ponce: Killing me Softly, but not the Fugees version.

Ned: It was the original by Roberta Flack, is that all that happened

Mr. Ponce: Yeah one of those little robots came out, but this one was a little different it had little speakers and a slim long knife strapped to it. On the side, it had two little mice painted on it with a circle and a line through them.

Ned: What did the little robot do?

Mr. Ponce: It started moving around, the mouse kept moving around, along the wall, every so often speeding up and putting the knife along the bottom. I think the robot was following the mouse. About this time, the mouse decided that was a good time to climb on top me. I tried to sweep the mouse away, but I just couldn't move because of the pain.

Ned: How did the robot react to the mouse climbing on top of you?

Mr. Ponce: It seemed to be looking for the mouse, then I heard the mouse squeak, and the little robot spun several times and slashed towards me. It missed but I could see how sharp the knife looked. The robot stayed close to me and began searching again.

Ned: What did you do?

Mr. Ponce: What did I do? Nothing I tried not to move, not to breath, the mouse was on my shoulder, and the little robot was searching. I didn't know what else to do.

Ned: Did it work?

Mr. Ponce: It did seem like it did, the mouse sat there, and the robot searched, but didn't get any closer. The mouse crept on to the side of my head, I was afraid to move.

Ned: Did the mouse stay there or move?

Mr. Ponce: It squeaked, the robot spun into me, the knife was very sharp.

Ned: You died by Roomba?

Mr. Ponce: Yes, I died by Roomba.

Ned: Because you have been cooperative. I am going to go ahead and break the rules and tell you what my recommendation will be. As you know the traditional punishment is the Eighth ring treatment, and most do not understand what is happening hindering the damnation.

Mr. Ponce: Yes, I had no idea for those 50 years what was happening.

Ned: Yes, that is a problem for most, but since you now know what the punishment is for, I am recommending the Eighth Circle of Hell damnation.

Damnation recommendation:

Recommend the Eighth Circle of Hell damnation, damnation review in two-thousand years.

DOCUMENT 12

INTERVIEW: 347440-7895645

Interview: 347440-7895645

Demon: John-859753-45*e4

<u>Soul</u>

Given Name: Jeffery Allen Hershell

Also Known as: Hershy

Occupation: none

Transcribed by: Demon Transcriber #0907987876765-3457a3b

Transcript

John-859753-45*e4 (From here on referred to as "John ".): It is my job to interview you to determine your damnation status and/or clarification of specifics of your level of damnation in Hell.

Jeffery Allen Hershell: (From here on referred to as "Mr. Hershel".): Ah, hello.

John: State your full name.

Mr. Hershell: Jeffery Allen Hershell, where…where am I?

John: Mr. Hershell you are in Hell, I am here to clarify some specifics about the day you died.

Mr. Hershell: Wait, I am not dead, I am sitting here, in this room talking to you.

John: I am telling you that you are dead, also you have been damned to the confines of Hell.

Mr. Hershell: No way. Is someone playing a trick on me?

John: Do you remember how you got here? The river you crossed. The big boat you got in, the riverboat master Charon. Do you remember any of that?

Mr. Hershell: Oh yeah cool dude, kind of skinny though.

John: What about the three headed dog, goes by the name of Cerberus?

Mr. Hershell: Oh yeah, the dog in the costume.

John: Hellfire and brimstone all over the place, did not give you any clues?

Mr. Hershell: What's brimstone?

John: That sulfur smell.

Mr. Hershell: Oh okay...what's sulfur?

(John places his head in his hands.)

John: This is going to be a long interview.

Mr. Hershell: Can I ask a question?

John: Yes, ask your question.

Mr. Hershell: Why does everything smell like rotten eggs?

(John waves and a bottle of Johnny Walker Blue and a small glass with ice in it appears, John pours a double, drinks it, and pours another.)

John: It seems that you do not understand your current status as a damned soul in Hell.

(John looks at the wall to the side of the desk, a door appears.)

John: Maybe meeting some residents might convince you?

Mr. Hershell: Nice trick, is it a real door?

(The door opens, a man is standing in it. He is tall, pale, and has a mustache that goes all the way across his face.)

John: I would like to introduce you to Vlad the Impaler, also known as Vlad Dracula.

Mr. Hershell: Cool so is he named after the vampire?

John: It's the other way around.

Mr. Hershell: Wait, a made-up guy that is named after this guy. A really famous made up guy and this guy didn't sue, there's laws against that, I don't buy it.

(The door closes, and opens, a medium height man stands with dark balding hair, a mustache, small goatee and a woolen suit.)

John: I would like to introduce you to…

Mr. Hershell: Wait, I know this guy, it's Lenin.

John: Finally, you know someone that should be here?

Mr. Hershell: What would he be doing in hell, we had a statue in the park where I grew up, he was…what did they call him…oh yeah, a "glorious leader".

(John reaches and a file appears, he studies it for a few minutes.)

John: Well that explains it, you grew up in Seattle.

Mr. Hershell: Yeah, that is where I learned all the stuff I know.

John: I am not sure that is something you want to be proud of.

Mr. Hershell: But it's great, it's got coffee and...ah coffee.

(The door slams shut.)

John: Who would I have to show you to prove that you are dead?

Mr. Hershell: My mom, she died a few years ago.

John: I cannot do that, most single mothers get special consideration and do not end up in Hell. they spend a lot of time in a spa in purgatory that has margaritas, pina coladas, and pool boys in speedos.

Mr. Hershell: See you can't do that. I knew I wasn't dead.

John: What about your father, he is here?

Mr. Hershell: My father's not dead, he is in prison, and why would I want to see him?

(A door opens, a man in a business suit is standing there, he is screaming but making no sounds.)

Mr. Hershell: That's not my father.

John: Yes, it is, your mother desperately needed money for food, and her boss gave her extra money to be with him occasionally.

Mr. Hershell: What? You are lying!

John: Demons cannot lie, Truth works better as a form of torture than lies.

Mr. Hershell: You are not a demon, you don't have horns, you're not red and you don't have a tail.

John: That is really a wrong stereotype, not all demons have horns, and we are not all red.

Mr. Hershell: What about the tail?

(John's prehensile tail snaps under the table and wraps Mr. Hershell several times, picks him up and slams him against the wall.)

John: I was trying not to torture you because you are mainly in Hell because your stupidity caused such pain in others. You are literally in Hell because you choose to be ignorant and stupid. The disrespect, pain, and anxiety you caused your mother alone was enough to get you put in Hell.

(John holding up the file.)

John: Look at this, on your twenty-second birthday you harassed your mother to buy you a gift, you said that you would not come and see her if she didn't.

(John's tail squeezes Mr. Hershell until he turns into mush, then drops him. John waves and Mr. Hershell heals and returns to the seat.)

Mr. Hershell: What kind of special effect did that? I thought I was being squeezed to death.

(John silently stares at Mr. Hershell.)

John: Why do you not believe you are in Hell?

Mr. Hershell: Well, no one officially told me I died.

John: That is why you don't believe you are in hell.

Mr. Hershell: Yeah, I mean I figured I would be told if I was dead.

John: Hold on.

(John reaches, a phone appears where he is reaching, he picks it up, and speaks into the phone.)

John: Have you been monitoring the interview, no, well can you review it real quick. Yes I can wait, no I don't have any ideas. Ok, well that does not seem like it makes sense, but I will try it.

(John hangs up the phone and it disappears.)

John: I can see the issue you are having, so we would like to correct some mistakes.

Mr. Hershell: ...Sure whatever you say.

(The door opens, a short balding man carrying a medical bag is standing there.)

John: Here is the medical examiner that announced your death.

(John speaking to the medical examiner.)

John: Sir, is Mr. Hershell dead?

Medical Examiner: Yes, there was not much left, but I can assure you, Mr. Jeffery Allen Hershell is dead.

(Door shuts, then opens, a very tall figure in black is standing there, holding a scythe.)

John: Sir, sorry to bother you, where did Mr. Hershell's soul end up after he died?

Death: No problem John he went to Hell.

(Door shuts, then opens, an almost cartoon figure stands there, red suit, red horns, red tail, and a red pitchfork. John quickly stands to attention.)

John: Sorry Sir, but it seemed like a solution, would you please tell us where is Mr. Hershell's soul now?

Satan: In my domain, Hell, where it belongs.

John: Thank you Sir, again sorry to bother you.

(Door shuts.)

Mr. Hershell: I am dead?

John: Yes, you are dead.

Mr. Hershell: I am in Hell?

John: Yes, you are in Hell.

Mr. Hershell: Why, why, why?

(Mr. Hershell begins crying and sobbing and screaming and then cries and sobs more.)

John: Let us take a break.

Interview stops for fifty-five-years, and two days.

John: I see you have finally accepted you are in dead and in Hell.

Mr. Hershell: Yeah, I have accepted it.

John: Good, now we can move on to the questions I have about your last day alive, what do you remember about.

Mr. Hershell: Well, it was a day, nothing that I can remember that made it special.

John: You were supposed to go on a date, with a girl, I believe her name was, oh yes, Tina.

Mr. Hershell: Yeah, she worked at the gas station where I would buy my lotto tickets.

John: Was there anything special about her?

Mr. Hershell: Yeah, Tina, she had a thing for animals, she was always wearing these shirts with like tigers and bears on them.

John: Did this affect your plans for the date?

Mr. Hershell: Not really, I was gonna take her to the burger place down the road, and then back to my room.

John: When you say your room, do you mean you had your own place?

Mr. Hershell: No man, Buggy is cool enough to let me stay over his garage, no air or bathroom but I can't beat the price.

John: Is that what happened?

Mr. Hershell: Well, I was down in Buggy's house trying to borrow a shirt, he told me that Tina really likes animals, and that I should take her to the zoo. It seemed like a good idea, she was wearing those animal shirts all the time; she might like that better than my room.

John: I would assume so. Did you get tickets to the zoo?

Mr. Hershell: I tried, but they wanted like thirty-five dollars apiece for us to get in. I didn't have that kind of money. But, I had a plan.

John: What was the plan?

Mr. Hershell: Well see, Tina didn't get off until like nine, but I found out the zoo closes at eight. I wanted to take her, 'cause well I heard that she got horny around animals and it had been too long since I, well you know.

John: Too long as in never.

Mr. Hershell: Yeah, never. But this was my chance. All I had to do was get us in the zoo, at night and we would have the run of the place, you know "like lions, tigers, and bears oh my". Something like that, but I didn't want to be anywhere close to the lions, tigers and bears.

John: Did you find a way in?

Mr. Hershell: I borrowed Buggy's car he was really nice about it, said "I needed to find someone to live with, and Tina would do". He usually says no. So anyway, I drove all around the zoo looking for a way in, they had roads but the entire place had a wall around it. I couldn't find any place to get in. I was not having any luck

John: How did you solve the problem?

Mr. Hershell: I was about to say "fuck it" when I saw a power crew working?

John: A power crew?

Mr. Hershell: The power crewman, they fix the lights and power things.

John: How did seeing the power crew help?

Mr. Hershell: They had a ladder, a big one; it was big enough for me to get over the wall.

John: Did you decide to go find a ladder?

Mr. Hershell: Why would I do that? I just waited until they took a break, grabbed their ladder, threw it on the car top and drove around back to the zoo. But I kind of screwed up, I dented Buggy's roof with the ladder.

John: Well, you will not have to deal with him.

Mr. Hershell: True man, true, anyway I got around back. It was getting dark; I thought to myself I need to get this set before it gets dark, no reason to be stupid.

John: Agreed, no reason to be stupid. Did you get it set up?

Mr. Hershell: Yep, sat it up in a nice, secluded spot. It was a high, but no problem; I had this.

John: It seems like you had it under control, did you go get Tina?

Mr. Hershell: Oh yeah picked her up, told her not to ask where we were going. I even grabbed a six-pack for us to share.

John: You are such a gentleman; did she like the zoo?

Mr. Hershell: Would you believe she wouldn't climb the ladder? I know it was a little dark but I had a flashlight. She was just being a stuck-up bitch.

John: Did you give up going to the zoo?

Mr. Hershell: No man, I told her I would show her how safe it was. So, I climbed the ladder, but there was wire at the top of it. No problem I told her, I climbed back down, got in Buggy's car and got some bolt cutters.

John: I am glad to find out you were prepared.

Mr. Hershell: I sure was, so I climbed back to the top, and started cutting the wire. No problemo, I had this.

John: Did the wire cutting go the way you planned?

Mr. Hershell: Not really, well see I wanted to make sure there were no wires to bother Tina when I talked her into climbing over. I reached as far as I could to the left and right, then I wanted to cut the ones at the top, but I couldn't get to it the way I wanted from the ladder.

John: How did you decide to get the ones at the top?

Mr. Hershell: I stood on the top of the wall. It wasn't wide, but I am good at balancing.

John: Did you get the wires cut?

Mr. Hershell: I fell.

John: Inside or outside of the Zoo?

Mr. Hershell: Inside, I fell inside the zoo, in water.

John: You fell inside the zoo, in water. Were you hurt?

Mr. Hershell: Not really, I was a little beat up and wet.

John: What did you do then?

Mr. Hershell: I needed to get out, so I started looking around.

John: Why didn't you use your planned way out?

Mr. Hershell: I hadn't really figured that out yet.

John: Okay, so you didn't have a plan to get out.

Mr. Hershell: Yeah, a little hiccup with that.

John: Please continue, what happened then?

Mr. Hershell: I was getting cold, the water was freezing, so I started looking for a way out of the water. I went one way and the water got deep, I am not a good swimmer, but I made it back to something to stand on.

John: Could you see or hear anything?

Mr. Hershell: It was dark, there were lights, but they were too far away to help. All I heard was Tina yelling if I was ok. I decided to ignore her, anyway she is the one that caused this.

John: Tell me what your actions were.

Mr. Hershell: I was getting colder, it felt like that they had the air blowing, but it was outside. Why would they do that? Well anyway, I started feeling my way around. Until I made my way out of the water, by now I was freezing. I was starting to shake, I needed to get out of the wet clothes. I dropped my pants and sat down on the ground to take off my shoes.

John: Did that help?

Mr. Hershell: No, when I sat down, I found ice, there was fucking ice on the ground. I mean it's fucking August and there's fucking ice on the ground.

John: Was the ground frozen?

Mr. Hershell: No, someone had poured ice all over the ground. There must have been a twelve-foot section full of ice.

John: Did you make it off the ice?

Mr. Hershell: Oh yeah, I was freezing and I had to move, I started moving to the lights, I stumbled but I made it to a big ditch. I couldn't see the bottom, but it was deep. No way I could get across, it must have been twelve-foot wide.

Document I2 Interview: 347440-7895645

John: How did you continue?

Mr. Hershell: I followed the ditch to a wall, but I couldn't get up that wall either.

John: I want to make sure I have this correct. You were in the zoo, freezing in August, you had fallen in freezing water, found an extremely deep ditch, and were you beginning to worry?

Mr. Hershell: Why? They keep those animals pretty drugged up. I saw it on a TV show.

John: I am glad you are so informed, please continue.

Mr. Hershell: I couldn't get over the ditch, and I couldn't go up the wall, I was thinking that there must be a door here somewhere. I started walking along the wall looking for anything that would help.

John: Did you find a door?

Mr. Hershell: Yep I found a door, well where a door usually goes. I found a big hole in the wall instead.

John: Did you go in?

Mr. Hershell: What choice did I have? I was freezing, if nothing else I might find something to keep me warm.

John: What did you find in the hole?

Mr. Hershell: Something that was furry, I was going along the wall; I couldn't see anything, until I found a wall of fur.

John: What did you do?

Mr. Hershell: I ran, I took off as fast as my feet would go, right into another fur wall. I remember thinking "Why a fur wall?"

John: Do you remember anything else?

Mr. Hershell: I remember hearing a splash, and that is the last thing I remember.

Afternote: The swipe from the polar bear moved Mr. Hershell from where he was standing to the wall, the splash was Mr. Hershell falling from the wall to the water. The polar bears had an extra treat to eat that night.

Damnation recommendation:

Recommend Mr. Hershell is the pieces of quilt for a quilting circle for grandmothers who children and grandchildren do not visit. He is to be able to hear and feel everything but unable to interact. Reset every morning. At night, he is to be transformed into a seal, surrounded by hungry polar bears, reset every hour. Damnation review in five-hundred years.

Damnation adjustment:

Every other night Mr. Hershell is a seal for
playful orcas. Damnation review extended another
five-hundred years.

DOCUMENT 13

INTERVIEW: 1999085AS

Interview: I999085as

Demon: Stacy-780376-9876*e4

<u>Soul</u>

Given Name: Walter Edward Martin

Also Known as: Walt

Occupation: Petty Thief

Transcribed by: Demon Transcriber #0907987876765-3457a3b

Transcript

Stacy-780376-9876*e4 (From here on referred to as "Stacy".): It is my job to interview you to determine your damnation status and/or clarification of specifics of your level of damnation in Hell.

Walter Edward Martin (From here on referred to as "Mr. Martin".): Screw you Bitch.

Stacy: I see I am going to have to correct your first impression of me on your weak ass.

(Stacy waves her hand, Mr. Martin is flung against the wall. Straps grab his arms and legs locking him to the wall.)

Mr. Martin: What the hell is this, trying to show off for one of your male co-workers? Or am I up here so you can give me a blowjob?

Stacy: Obviously, you do not understand the situation you are in. I am going to take some time to clarify the misunderstanding. As I am a student of human history, I like to take from the cruel human race. Do you like animals?

(A bucket appears in front of Mr. Martin. Five small rats appear and drop into the bucket, which snaps onto Mr. Martins belly.)

Mr. Martin: Screw you, rats don't bother me.

Stacy: You do not read much, do you Mr. Martin? The rats are no problem, until heat is applied then they try to rip their way out, through the only available place, your stomach. Because you have been so polite, I have made it so that your stomach heals just enough to keep the rats busy, for a very long time. Enjoy.

(A lit torch appears hanging in front of the bucket, applying the flame to the bottom of the bucket.)

Mr. Martin: Fuck you…

(A gag appears in Mr. Martin's mouth, he starts struggling, and chewing noises can be heard.)

Stacy: That should keep you busy for a while.

(Stacy waves again, a Martini and book appears on the table, she picks up both, and begins reading.)

Interview stops for four years, five months and three days

Document I3 Interview: I999085as

Stacy: That was a nice little break.

(Stacy waves, the bucket disappears, and Mr. Martin moves to the chair.)

Mr. Martin: How…how…how did you do that?

Stacy: You are in Hell.

Mr. Martin: I mean how could you be so cruel? It's inhuman.

Stacy: What part of Demon do you not understand?

Mr. Martin: You let me hang on the wall being eaten by rats for years? How is that fair?

Stacy: Fair, in Hell? I need to check your psychological evaluation.

(Stacy reaches, a file appears in her hand.)

Stacy: That explains it, you passed but you are a sexist piece of shit, who refuses to accept anything that you do not understand.

Mr. Martin: Fuck you I didn't take any fucking exam or whatever the fuck you are talking about.

Stacy: You do not have to take anything, we know. Now to adjust your point of view on your situation.

(Chains come out of the walls grabbing Mr. Martin's arms and legs pulling him into a spread-eagle position. The table and chairs disappear leaving a bare room with just Mr. Martin hanging.

Stacy begins walking slowly back and forth in front of Mr. Martin.)

Mr. Martin: Put me down you fucking dyke.

(Stacy reaches out and rips Mr. Martin's tongue out.)

Stacy: You will not need that for a while. Have you ever seen the movie Hellraiser? We consider it a classic comedy, but it has some really good ideas. As I have said, I love to take from human ideas and use them. Just a little quirk I have discovered, it works well, humans are so creative.

(Mr. Martin moans and nods no.)

Stacy: Oh, you have not? Well the next few years should be very informative for you. I am going to give you a lesson on human cruelty and how inventive humans can be when it comes to the evil they do to other humans.

(Mr. Martin begins moaning and shaking his head vigorously side to side.)

Stacy: We are going to start with my favorite scene from Hellraiser. In the movie, chains come out and rip a guy apart. It was good, but they didn't use enough chains and they did it too quickly. I will adjust it for you.

(A chain comes out from the wall and hooks on to Mr. Martin's abdomen, followed by another, and another until his entire body is hooked by the chains.)

Document I3 Interview: I999085as

Stacy: After I finish with my favorite scene, I think we will go down the entire list of death scenes of horror movies from the I980's. Are you familiar with Freddy, Jason, and Chucky? You will be.

(The chains start to pull slowly on the skin, pulling the skin from the body.)

Stacy: I also have a rewind button.

(The chains reverse just enough to put the skin almost to the body, then pulls again)

Stacy: This is going to be a real good time.

(For the next ten years, Mr. Martin experienced every death scene in all five-hundred-eighty-two horror movies released in the United States during the I980s. Some scenes were repeated as many as fifteen times.)

Stacy: Now that I have shown you how cruel the human mind can be, I hope that you will be more forthcoming with the information we need.

(Mr. Martin's tongue is restored.)

Mr. Martin: ….Chucky…why Chucky…

Stacy: Are you going to give the information?

Mr. Martin: Yes, yes, oh god yes.

Stacy: Yes what?

Mr. Martin: Yes Ma'am

Document I3 Interview: I999085as

Stacy: Now State your full name.

Mr. Martin: Walter…Walter Martin…Walter Edward Martin.

Stacy: Glad you are finally learning. Now Mr. Martin we are interested in your last day on Earth. Specifically, why you choose to rob the place you did. Tell me about the place you choose to rob.

Mr. Martin: Yes, anything, I specialized in robbing conventions, meetings, any event that had, I guess you would call them easy targets, especially if the money looked good. I was casing a hotel for a big job in two weeks, a semi-precious stone event; they sometimes have some precious stones. While I was casing the joint I realized there was an event for that night. It was a kind of military thing.

Stacy: What made you realize there was a military event happening that night?

Mr. Martin: There were some guys there practicing with flags, marching up and down. Seemed odd, but who am I to judge. I heard them talking about how excited they were to meet these guys. Must have been some big shots or something. Big shots are always good for a quick score.

Stacy: You did not know what the event was or who the big shots were.

Mr. Martin: I didn't have a clue what it was. Something about honoring MOH recipients, but it must have been some kind of big deal. I decided to scout out that event, and there were four different TV stations there. That sealed it, I knew I had to hit them.

Stacy: Did the Television crews worry you?

Mr. Martin: Not at all, they rarely see what is in front of their face.

Stacy: So how did you proceed?

Mr. Martin: I looked around and got the feel of the place. It didn't seem like it was a big event, they only had one room reserved. It was a large one, but still only one room. I called to make a reservation, but the hotel was booked solid, it didn't really add up.

Stacy: Why did it not add up?

Mr. Martin: They had only one room booked, but they had seven cash bars planned.

Stacy: Is that a lot?

Mr. Martin: Yeah, the last three I hit had only two for each room. They had seven planned for one room.

Stacy: Did this look like a promising opportunity?

Mr. Martin: Hell yell, the bars alone made it worth it. But they also seemed to have some special decorations coming in. The bus boy was

Document I3 Interview: I999085as

complaining about it during a smoke break. I mean only big events bring their own stuff. I was getting excited, I had to come up with a good plan, and normally the big events like this have lots of security. I started looking around but didn't see a lot of security. This was looking better and better.

Stacy: Did you come up with a plan?

Mr. Martin: I didn't have a lot of time, but yeah, I came up with a pretty good plan.

Stacy: What was your plan?

Mr. Martin: I had to call a few buddies and make it quick. Simple is usually the best. We had five guys in the crew now. We would wait until halfway through the night, we were to go in through separate doors, hit the cash bars, and a few big shots. Head out before they know what happened. Most people don't realize how disorienting a fast robbery can make people.

Stacy: Did it go as planned?

Mr. Martin: It started off good, I was watching to see how often they were refilling the bars. I have to say whoever they were they could drink. I've never seen so many bottles of whiskey going into an event. Those cash bars must have been making a killing. I couldn't wait to see how much this was gonna get us.

Stacy: When did it start to go wrong?

Mr. Martin: I kept waiting for the big shots to show up. Usually it's easy to see, some assholes pull up in a limo, or come down a hall with an entourage a mile long. I must have missed it because the ceremony started. I snuck a peak in and a lot of them were in uniform. Maybe some kind of formal thing I saw some guys in tuxedos. But all different, I didn't know what to make of it. We just had to pick the right time.

Stacy: When did that time happen?

Mr. Martin: I was waiting on the big shots but they never seemed to show up. The only thing I saw was a mix of guys who came in shortly after the event started. Mostly old guys with canes, some in wheelchairs, a few young guys. I couldn't tell what the fuck was going on. But they must have been something, everyone in the room was making a big deal out of them. You would have thought they were celebrities or something.

Stacy: I am sure there was something special about them. When did you decide to begin the robbery?

Mr. Martin: The night was starting to get late You don't want to wait too long. They start taking the cash from the bars to "secure" it. About 9:45pm I went ahead and texted the other guys we would hit them at I0pm on the dot. Then I moved to a little alcove a few feet from the door I was supposed to go through, that is when the entire night went to hell.

Stacy: What happened?

Mr. Martin: There was some old guy with a cane standing in the alcove, smoking a cigar. Can you believe he was smoking a cigar inside? Who did he think he was?

Stacy: I would not hazard a guess.

Mr. Martin: I told him he needed to put it out. Do you know what he said? He told me to "Fuck off, pencil dick" and that he "would smoke anywhere he damn well pleased".

Stacy: How did you react?

Mr. Martin: I couldn't react, we were about to burst through the doors in like one minute. I just made a mental note to pistol whip him on the way out.

Stacy: Did you bust through the door?

Mr. Martin: Did I? I was still pissed at the old fucker, so I kicked the shit out of that door. Walked into the front of their ceremony pointed my gun at a guy in a wheelchair and told them we were gonna take all their money.

Stacy: What kind of reaction did you get?

Mr. Martin: You know that's the odd thing, when you point your gun at most people they react, they either shake, cry, get pissed off or something. This old guy just took a puff from a pipe, nothing else, he acted like I didn't have a gun.

Document I3 Interview: I999085as

Stacy: What did you do?

Mr. Martin: I told them that if they didn't do exactly what I said I would shoot the old guy.

Stacy: How did they respond?

Mr. Martin: The old guy I was pointing my gun at said "You ain't got the balls" and took another puff on his pipe.

Stacy: Did you respond to him?

Mr. Martin: To be honest his lack of reaction was getting a little spooky, but I had to do something. I told him "I will shoot, you old goat".

Stacy: How did he respond?

Mr. Martin: He looked at me and said, "Go on if you got the balls, you won't be the first to shoot me, asshole".

Stacy: Did you shoot?

Mr. Martin: Yeah, I shot…I shot his wheelchair.

Stacy: You shot his wheelchair?

Mr. Martin: Yeah, but the fucker just looked up and said, "See everyone, no balls." Then everyone laughed.

Stacy: Everyone laughed? Is that all?

Mr. Martin: Then a guy with a cane, you know the cane with the tennis balls on the bottom. He yelled to the guy in the wheelchair, "You're right, these young fuckers have no balls." And everyone laughed again. I was starting to worry.

Stacy: Why were you worrying?

Mr. Martin: They were not reacting right. They were acting like I wasn't scary at all.

Stacy: You were supposed to be scary?

Mr. Martin: Yeah, I had the gun.

Stacy: Did you think you had the only gun in the room?

Mr. Martin: Yeah, I thought the I had the only one. What kind of people go to a party with guns?

Stacy: Maybe the kind of people you don't want to try and rob? Were you correct about having the only gun?

Mr. Martin: No, the guy in the wheelchair shot me.

Stacy: He shot you, where did he shoot you?

Mr. Martin: In the leg?

Stacy: He shot you in the leg? What happened then?

Mr. Martin: All the other guys started yelling insults at him.

Stacy: Insults, what do you mean.

Mr. Martin: I didn't understand most of them. They said things, like "you need range time," "center mass", and the one I really didn't understand "you missed you fucking leg." I didn't understand the last one at all. I mean he hit me in the leg, but they seemed to be calling him a leg.

Stacy: Did you think you were still scary at this point?

Mr. Martin: No, I was getting scared, something about the way the old guy reacted to being called a leg.

Stacy: How did he react?

Mr. Martin: He just got a look on his face. He looked pissed. He said something about "Just not wanting to kill, again." Wonder what he meant by again?

Stacy: What did you do?

Mr. Martin: I needed to get out of there, I started limping towards the door.

Stacy: Wait you were running from a ninety plus year old man in a wheelchair?

Mr. Martin: Well yeah, he just shot me!

Stacy: But you still had a gun, correct?

Mr. Martin: Yeah, but you don't understand, he was pissed.

Stacy: You were supposed to scare them and take the money right?

Mr. Martin: Fuck that I needed out of there.

Stacy: What about your friends that were supposed to be helping?

Mr. Martin: I saw one of them on the floor. He was bleeding. A guy in a blue uniform and a black cowboy hat standing over him with a sword. I mean WHAT THE FUCK, where did he get a fucking sword?

Stacy: Did you make it out?

Mr. Martin: Hell no, three of the younger guys were blocking the door.

Stacy: How did you react?

Mr. Martin: I pointed my gun at them and said, "Move motherfuckers, I will shoot you!".

Stacy: Did they move?

Mr. Martin: I think the old guy in the wheelchair shot me in the shoulder. I felt pain in my shoulder and dropped my gun.

Stacy: You dropped your gun and then what?

Mr. Martin: I grabbed my switchblade and said I would slash their throats for getting in my way. Then it got really scary.

Stacy: How did it get scary?

Mr. Martin: One of the guys standing off to the side started talking.

Stacy: What did he start talking about?

Mr. Martin: He told me I was about to become "a fucking late term abortion" and that I didn't know how to hold a fucking knife. Then he started talking about how to kill someone, but it didn't make sense. He said, "you don't slash a throat, you stab it from the side.".

Stacy: Did that scare you?

Mr. Martin: Hell yeah, he was talking real soft, but it was like it was a fact, like he knew exactly what he was talking about.

Stacy: For the record he did. Did he say anything else?

Mr. Martin: Yeah, he said someone should demonstrate.

Stacy: How did you react?

Mr. Martin: I don't remember reacting just a pain in the side of my neck, and a big ass bloody dagger in front of my face.

Stacy: Is that all you remember?

Mr. Martin: No, the last thing I remember is someone saying, "Like that?"

Damnation recommendation:

Recommend Mr. Martin spend time as the 50 meter "Ivan", the green silhouette that is used on rifle ranges in the United States Army, feeling every shot, unable to communicate. Damnation review in five-hundred-fifty years.

DOCUMENT 14

INTERVIEW: 7987668A

Interview: 7987668a

Demon: Jim-9876839763*e4

<u>Soul</u>

Given Name: William Walter Jones

Also Known as: none

Occupation: Remake Movie Producer

Transcribed by: Demon Transcriber #0907987876765-3457a3b

Transcript

Jim-9876839763*e4 (From here on referred to as "Jim".): It is my job to interview you to determine your damnation status and/or clarification of specifics of your level of damnation in Hell.

William Walter Jones (From here on referred to as "Mr. Jones".): Where am I?

Jim: You are in Hell, state your full name.

Mr. Jones: William Walter Jones, I am kind of a big deal, you may have heard of me.

Jim: Why would I have heard of you?

Mr. Jones: I make movies.

Jim: What are some of the movies you have made?

Mr. Jones: I remade…

(Jim grabs him by the throat and slams him to the wall.)

Jim: You remake movies? This must be my lucky day.

Mr. Jones: Don't you like movies?

Jim: I love movies; I mean I really love movies.

Mr. Jones: Then why are you choking me, I make movies?

Jim: What original movies do you make?

Mr. Jones: I only do remakes.

(Jim begins to slam Mr. Jones' head on the wall, then begins hitting him.)

Jim: Remakes are the lowest forms of movies; you take someone else's creative idea and suck the life out of it. I must be performing my job well for them to send me a loser like you. I suggest you get used to the torture. I am sure that the demons are going to want to meet you.

Mr. Jones: Why…

(Jim waves and a large meat grinder appears. He takes Mr. Jones and starts feeding him into it, grinding slowly. Jim smiling from ear to ear. Jim grinds Mr. Jones completely into a pile of ground meat. Heals him, grinds him, and repeats for the next twenty years.)

Interview resumes after twenty years.

Document I4 Interview: 7987668a

Jim: Mr. Jones, I am so glad you came into my interview room, I must say I will enjoy assigning your damnation. I have learned to enjoy the little things.

Mr. Jones: Why, why did you do that?

Jim: Just for my own personal enjoyment.

Mr. Jones: Please, I just remade…

(Jim reaches out and pokes Mr. Jones in the eyes, his fingers going through the back of his head.)

Jim: I must thank the assignment demons for this.

Mr. Jones: I can't see. How am I supposed to be interviewed?

Jim: You do not need your eyes to be interviewed. We are interested in your last day on earth, do you remember that day?

Mr. Jones: I think I do. I was in my office looking for my next rema…my next movie.

Jim: How were you looking?

Mr. Jones: I was surfing the net.

Jim: Did anything unusual happen?

Mr. Jones: Not really, my lawyer called and told me we were being sued again, copyright violation.

Jim: Does that happen a lot?

Mr. Jones: Weekly, we have an entire department set aside for that.

Jim: Nothing else happened?

Mr. Jones: I was supposed to see one of the writers we use to rewrite the movies.

Jim: One of the hack writers that destroy classics?

(Jim reaches out and rips one of Mr. Jones' fingers off. Mr. Jones screams.)

Jim: What was the conversation about?

Mr. Jones: He was supposed to have finished a rewrite but was late, he was drunk again complaining about being original; he wanted to add things as usual, or something of that nature.

Jim: Originality, you mean destroying classics.

Mr. Jones: We make them better.

(Jim reaches out and rips another finger off, Mr. Jones screams again.)

Jim: No, you destroy them; we all know that you just want money.

Mr. Jones: Why do you keep hurting me?

Jim: Personal enjoyment, pure and simple. Now back to your day, so you talked to a writer. What happened after that?

Mr. Jones: I am not sure I want to answer that question.

Jim: Please do not answer, I want to motivate you to cooperate.

Mr. Jones: What do you mean?

Jim: Not cooperating no problem, time to make you cooperate. Do you like pirate movies? I love them.

(The interview is moved to the top of a pirate ship. Mr. Jones eyes are healed.)

Mr. Jones: What are we doing here?

Jim: Are you familiar with "Keel-Hauling"?

Mr. Jones: I know that people say stuff like do that and we will keel-haul you.

Jim: Didn't you make a pirate movie where they keel-hauled several characters?

Mr. Jones: Maybe I don't really pay attention to the actual movies.

Jim: It shows. Keel-Hauling takes the person who is being punished. Running a rope under the keel of the ship, hooking it to the person, and pulling under the keel. They are pulled along the bottom of the boat where barnacles are. It rips the skin off slowly, most people die. It is particularly brutal and violent. The survivors are scarred horribly.

Mr. Jones: That sounds horrible.

Document I4 Interview: 7987668a

Jim: It is.

(A rope grabs both of Mr. Jones legs, guides itself under the ship, comes up the other side and grabs his arms.)

Jim: I think I am going to enjoy this.

(A flask of spice rum appears in Jim's hand. The rope starts pulling Mr. Jones over the side, Mr. Jones begins screaming. A while later Mr. Jones appears on the other side of the ship and is pulled onto the deck. He is bloody and beat up.)

Jim: It is so nice that you cannot die in Hell.

Mr. Jones: I…I cannot die?

Jim: How many movies did you remake?

Mr. Jones: I…I remade…I remade twenty-seven movies.

Jim: That is the number we will use.

Mr. Jones: I…I …I have… to do that twenty-seven times.

Jim: No that would be silly and we don't do silly things what do you think this is Monty Python, no of course don't have to to do that twenty-seven times.

Mr. Jones: Oh, thank lord.

Jim: You have to do it for twenty-seven years.

(The rope begins to pull Mr. Jones under the boat. Mr. Jones begins screaming. Jim waves and a TV begins playing a pirate movie. He sits and drinks from the flask.)

Twenty-seven years later.

(Jim and Mr. Jones appear in the interview room. Mr. Jones is healed just enough to continue the interview.)

Jim: Now are you willing to cooperate?

Mr. Jones: Yes, I will, God yes.

Jim: Are you sure you want to cooperate? I would not mind providing more motivation.

Mr. Jones: I will cooperate in any way you want.

Jim: Damn. So much for my fun, on with the interview. Continue with your day.

Mr. Jones: That evening I had a meeting on the next movie I was gonna…do. I took the client to a nice little restaurant to butter them up. I really needed them to sign over the rights to the movie. It was gonna be epic.

Jim: I am pretty sure it would not be an epic movie. Did you convince them to sign over the movie rights?

Mr. Jones: No, it seems there was a rumor about people wanting to remake the movie. Social media went nuts over it. I hate those losers on there, always screwing up my ideas.

Document I4 Interview: 7987668a

Jim: The people on social media didn't like what you wanted to do. Did that make you reconsider?

Mr. Jones: Never has before and it didn't that time either.

Jim: But the person you were meeting with had some concerns.

Mr. Jones: Yeah, she was being stubborn, I was offering a ton of money but she kept saying no.

Jim: Did this continue long?

Mr. Jones: She actually had the cojanes to try to leave.

Jim: Imagine her trying to express free will.

Mr. Jones: Exactly, didn't she realize who I was, she walked out of the restaurant. I had to follow. We were in the street, she started walking, I followed.

Jim: Did you think you were scaring her?

Mr. Jones: I hoped I was, it wouldn't be the first time I scared someone into signing over the rights.

Jim: Such a big man, intimating people to give up and sign.

Mr. Jones: But I got them to sign that was what was important.

Jim: Just go on with your last night on earth.

Mr. Jones: She is walking and refusing to talk. I was following her. I got lucky she came to a street crossing and had to stop. By this time, I was getting angry, I was talking, but I knew it was gonna go to the lawyers, I wanted the movie. People loved the original, and we could do nothing but improve it.

Jim: I do not believe that is correct. But go on.

Mr. Jones: There she was, standing on a corner, she had started crying and she just said "No, just no!"

Jim: How did you react?

Mr. Jones: I stepped in front of her, and I grabbed her by the arm, and yelled.

Jim: You grabbed her?

Mr. Jones: I was pissed off. That is when she sprayed me with pepper spray. That stuff burns.

Jim: What happened then?

Mr. Jones: I started stepping backwards, rubbing my eyes.

Jim: Do you remember what happened next?

Mr. Jones: A bus, I got hit by a bus.

Jim: Yes, you were killed by a bus.

Mr. Jones: Can you imagine someone like me hit by a bus?

Document I4 Interview: 7987668a

Jim: Yes, I can many, many times. By the way, what were your last words?

Mr. Jones: My last words were "Can you imagine, the Princess Bride in Space."

Damnation Recommendation:

Recommend Mr. Jones is fed to the rodents of unusual size, every morning, noon, and night. In between he must watch the Barney TV show, The Garbage Pail Kids movie, Reefer Madness, and from Justin to Kelly. Damnation review in two-hundred-thousand years.

Damnation Adjustment:

After review the damnation was considered not strong enough, waiting on a worse torture but none has presented itself.

DOCUMENT 15

INTERVIEW: 78987654-8A

Interview: 78987654-8a

Demon: Marvin-987009654*e4

<u>Soul</u>

Given Name: Jason Perry Wilson

Also Known as: none

Occupation: Musician (failed)

Transcribed by: Demon Transcriber #09079878767653457a3b

Transcript

Marvin-987009654*e4 (From here on referred to as "Marvin".): It is my job to interview you to determine your damnation status and/or clarification of specifics of your level of damnation in Hell.

Jason Perry Wilson (From here on referred to as "Mr. Wilson".): What in the hell is going on here?

Marvin: You have the Hell part right. I am here to clarify a few things about your damnation.

Mr. Wilson: Damnation? As in Hell? As in, I am dead?

Marvin: Yes, you are dead. State your full name so we may proceed with the interview.

Mr. Wilson: I am dead, man I didn't expect that.

Marvin: Your full name, now.

Mr. Wilson: Hold your horses; I am getting a grip on being dead.

Marvin: Allow me to assist you.

(Marvin waves and metal cuffs appear on Mr. Wilson's ankles and wrist. Chains lead in four different directions. Loud neighs come from the four directions.)

Mr. Wilson: What the fuck is this shit?

Marvin: You told me to hold my horses; I do not believe I will.

(Blows, snorts, and neighs come from the four directions. Snapping whip sounds soon fill the room. The chains snap tight, Mr. Wilson is quickly pulled apart.)

Marvin: That was not quartering, those pieces are not proportional, let's do that again.

(The room starts moving in reverse, Mr. Wilson is pushed back together.)

Marvin: Try again.

(Horses pull Mr. Wilson apart.)

Marvin: Not proportional, again.

(Room reversed. Mr. Wilson is back together.)

Marvin: Again.

(Horses pull Mr. Wilson apart.)

Marvin: Well shit.

(Room reversed. Mr. Wilson is back together.)

Marvin: Maybe if I help it along.

(Marvin walks over to Mr. Wilson, reaches up, a small scalpel appears in his hand. Marvin cuts small nicks dividing Mr. Wilson into four pieces. Mr. Wilson screams wildly)

Marvin: Again.

(Horses pull Mr. Wilson apart.)

Marvin: Closer.

(Room reversed, Mr. Wilson is back together, Marvin breathes a deep satisfied sigh, makes deeper cuts into Mr. Wilson.)

Marvin: I could do this all night.

(Marvin continues to pull Mr. Wilson apart, and putting him back together testing different techniques on how to quarter evenly. This activity goes on for seven days and six nights. Until Marvin accomplished a perfect quartering of Mr. Wilson.)

Marvin: Sometimes you just must do things until you figure out how to do them correctly. Would you say that is correct?

(Mr. Wilson is healed, moved to a chair, and the cuffs disappear.)

Mr. Wilson: You...you...horses...you...horses...

(Horse neigh in the background, Mr. Wilson begins sobbing.)

Marvin: Yes, I used horses to demonstrate you are indeed dead, you are in Hell, and you are going to be punished. That is not in question. But I did ask you a question, and sometimes you must do things until they are correct. Do you have an answer?

Mr. Wilson: Yes...yes...you...you are correct.

Marvin: So glad to see you understand your situation. You also understand I like to get things correct even if it takes me years for decades. Now state your full name.

Mr. Wilson: Jason.

Marvin: Is that what I asked?

Mr. Wilson: Jason Perry Wilson, Jason Perry Wilson, Jason Perry Wilson, please don't rip me apart again.

Marvin: See it is not hard to answer questions correctly. Mr. Wilson, I am here to get information, I expect you to answer my questions and not cause me irritation. I do not want to adjust your attitude, but if I do it will be done perfectly. Do you understand?

Mr. Wilson: I guess so.

Marvin: That is a "yes" or "no" question.

Document I5 Interview: 78987654-8a

(Horses neigh in the background.)

Mr. Wilson: Yes, god yes, I understand.

Marvin: Do you remember the night you died?

Mr. Wilson: Yes, yes, I remember.

Marvin: Good, tell me about it.

Mr. Wilson: Ah, sir, what do you want to know about that night?

Marvin: You were outside of a museum, with your colleagues, what were you doing there.

Mr. Wilson: We were waiting to take a picture.

Marvin: Why were you waiting?

Mr. Wilson: That may take some explaining, do you know the greatest rock band ever, Iron Maiden?

Marvin: I know of an English Metal band that goes by that name.

Mr. Wilson: Yeah that's them, I have been following them since The Number of the Beast in 1982. I bet you guys loved that down here.

Marvin: Some demons did, others did not. What does the band Iron Maiden have to do with your actions that night? The band was…

(Marvin reaches for a file, it appears.)

Marvin: Two-thousand-eighty-two miles from your location.

Document I5 Interview: 78987654-8a

Mr. Wilson: There was this picture contest, if you win it you get to play on stage with Iron Maiden. It could be my big break and make me a rock star.

Marvin: A big break for a fifty-year-old rock musician?

Mr. Wilson: Yeah, I mean you never know when it is gonna happen, you gotta believe.

Marvin: From your present position, I can say with some assurance, you are not going to get a break to become a rock star.

Mr. Wilson: Oh, yeah.

Marvin: What does waiting outside a museum have to do with the picture?

Mr. Wilson: What I wanted to take a picture of was inside of the museum. I know that they would not let me take good pics while the museum was open, so we decided to break in. I mean it's a museum, not like anything is valuable inside.

Marvin: Tell me about your collaborators.

Mr. Wilson: Oh yeah, there is Becky, she is my girl, kind of a groupie, she's all about the music.

(Marvin consults the file.)

Marvin: Let me see, Rebecca Lynn Myers, also known as Becky, says she is fifty-five-years-old. You have a fifty-five-year-old groupie.

Mr. Wilson: Oh yeah, she has been on the scene for a little while.

Marvin: Yes, for a…oh my yes just a "little" while. What about the other collaborators?

Mr. Wilson: There was Tommy, I was teaching him guitar, and in return, he helped us out now and then.

(Marvin consults the file.)

Marvin: Thomas Nathan Towns, also known as Tommy, age 2I. What was he doing for you on that night?

Mr. Wilson: To be honest I don't get around as good as I used to, he was there if we needed him. Climb things, carry things, or to be a gopher.

Marvin: Gopher? Why would he be a small burrowing rodent?

Mr. Wilson: Gopher, as in go for this, go for that.

Marvin: Oh, a pun.

Mr. Wilson: A what?

Marvin: A play on words, in this case the two sound alike, "gopher" and "go for."

Mr. Wilson: Oh, I didn't realize there was a name for it.

Marvin: There was one more collaborator.

Mr. Wilson: Oh you men Johnny Boy, he was gonna be our lookout.

(Marvin consults the file.)

Marvin: John James Boi, age fifty-one, also known as "Johnny Boy". How very original. It says here that he had severe damage from…

(Marvin consults the file.)

Marvin: Trying to body surf a mosh pit and failing. Body surfing a mosh pit? That does not sound like an intelligent idea.

Mr. Wilson: It wasn't, that happened in I99I. Johnny Boi has never been the brightest bulb. Not sure his volume dial goes to ten.

Marvin: I am sure you are right. Now that we have your collaborators tell me what you remember from that night.

Mr. Wilson: Sure, Johnny Boy was to stay outside as a lookout. He wasn't good for much, after that mosh pit he was never the same. Earlier in the day we had found a side door. Tommy had snuck in and put a piece of tape over the lock, I saw that in a movie. Then all we had to do was wait until the place closed.

Marvin: A movie seems like a reliable source for information. Were you worried about security guards?

Mr. Wilson: Not really, there was one, but he didn't seem like anything to worry about. I don't think he even had a gun.

Marvin: Did the tape on the lock work?

Mr. Wilson: Hell, no. That security guard went and checked all the doors. He pulled off the tape.

Marvin: The tape did not work, surprising. What did you do to get in?

Mr. Wilson: We thought we were screwed. We were trying to come up with an idea. When Becky saw a working girl going towards the side door that we had put tape on.

Marvin: By working girl, you mean an Escort.

Mr. Wilson: No man, I mean a prostitute, woman who has sex for money.

Marvin: Escort is a nicer way to say prostitute. What does the escort have to do with getting inside of the museum?

Mr. Wilson: The "Escort" knocked on the side door, and the security guard answered and let her in. When the guard let her in, the door didn't close all the way.

Marvin: The guards' mistake helped you get in the door?

Mr. Wilson: That horny fucker let us in and didn't even notice. We snuck in easy as pie.

Marvin: Who was "We"?

Mr. Wilson: Me, Johnny and Becky.

Marvin: What happened when you got inside.

Mr. Wilson: We got inside the door, which was right beside the guardroom by the way.

Marvin: Was the guard occupied?

Mr. Wilson: I'll say he was watching the "Escort", who was on her knees. He wasn't going to notice us.

Marvin: The guard was occupied while the escort performed fellatio on him?

Mr. Wilson: What's fellatio?

Marvin: Fellatio is oral sex performed on the penis.

Mr. Wilson: Oh okay, well anyway we pretty much had a run of the place when she was…fellatioing him.

(Marvin facepalms for a few seconds.)

Marvin: How did you proceed?

Mr. Wilson: We started looking for things.

Marvin: Did you have a specific item you wanted a picture of?

Mr. Wilson: Oh yeah, I had a great idea; I wanted a picture of the iron maiden for the Iron Maiden Contest. Smart uh?

Marvin: I bet no one else thought of it.

Mr. Wilson: I was a shoe in to win.

Marvin: Did you find the iron maiden?

Mr. Wilson: Not at first, I didn't realize how big the museum was. We couldn't find anything.

Marvin: Explain what you mean.

Mr. Wilson: I couldn't find anything. All we were finding were animals and bones. We went around in circles.

Marvin: You were going around in circles?

Mr. Wilson: Yeah, we were lost.

Marvin: You got lost in the museum? What happened to change your situation?

Mr. Wilson: Becky found a map, and you know there are different museum sections. We were in the Natural History section.

Marvin: You were in the Natural History Area of the museum. I do not believe there is an iron maiden in that part.

Mr. Wilson: We figured that out. Tommy got on his phone and found out that we needed to get to the medieval display. It was in the European history section. I was about to give up, when Tommy found that we could get to it without going outside.

Marvin: How did you get from the Natural History section to the European History section?

Mr. Wilson: We had to go through a skywalk. It scared the shit out of me. It was all clear like glass, even the floor. It was dark, we couldn't see anything. We all turned on our phone flashlight, but it was still scary.

Marvin: Did you make it across the skywalk?

Mr. Wilson: Yeah finally, I was shaking by the time we got the door to the other building open.

Marvin: Were you in the European History section?

Mr. Wilson: No man, there was nothing but paintings and statues. Johnny said we had to go down two floors to the basement.

Marvin: Was it hard to get down to the basement?

Mr. Wilson: Not hard just long, the elevators were turned off. We had to find the stairs. Fuckers were behind a door, but we found it.

Marvin: You made it to the basement and medieval display.

Mr. Wilson: Finally, it took us all night. This picture was worth it.

Marvin: What did you find when you got there?

Mr. Wilson: Some sick shit, talk about weird, I guess it was some bondage thing they set up. Didn't think the museum did stuff like that.

Marvin: I do not believe you are correct on the exhibit being a "bondage" exhibit. Did you find the iron maiden?

Mr. Wilson: There was a little problem. I didn't know what an iron maiden was.

Marvin: Wait, you have followed the band Iron Maiden for 38 years, you are entering a picture contest where you came up with the idea of this picture. But you did not know what an iron maiden actually was?

Mr. Wilson: Yeah…I didn't know.

Marvin: Did you find out what it was?

Mr. Wilson: I played it as cool as I could, I just started walking around looking like I was into that sick shit. Becky was really interested in the stuff, Tommy just kept by this coffin looking thing with nails on the inside. I went all around looking for the name plate. But I couldn't find it. I knew it was there, Tommy had found it on his phone.

Marvin: Did you eventually find it?

Mr. Wilson: I was pissed I had walked around the entire floor, and I finally said fuck it. I turned around and went back to where Tommy was, beside the coffin thingy. Tommy was putting Becky in this thing, you bend over, you put your head and hands in. It locks you up.

Marvin: That is called a stocks.

Mr. Wilson: Weird name, any way Becky is locked in the…stocks. I walk up and she says "I'm not wearing any panties, y'all could do anything you want to me.". Before I could tell her, I wasn't into all that, I see it.

Marvin: What do you see?

Mr. Wilson: The sign on the coffin thing, it says "Iron Maiden." That fucker had been standing beside it the entire time.

Marvin: You mean Tommy.

Mr. Wilson: Yeah, the fucker, standing there the whole time talking up Becky. I was pissed.

Marvin: The twenty-one-year-old, Tommy, was talking up the fifty-five-year-old Becky. What did you do about it?

Mr. Wilson: Nothing, like I said I am not that good at moving around now.

Marvin: I am not surprised. How did you proceed to take the picture?

Mr. Wilson: I looked at the iron maiden. I figured the best shot was if I was inside. The doors to it were open, but not enough for me to squeeze inside, but Tommy said he could take off these blocks on the bottom of the doors and open them for me to get inside then make it look good for the picture.

Marvin: Is that what happened?

Mr. Wilson: In a way, Tommy took off in search of some tools. Becky was still locked in the stocks. She tried to talk me into taking her, but I told her I wasn't into that sick bondage shit. She was getting pissed off, told me if I didn't she would offer it to Tommy. What a bitch, she is supposed to be my groupie.

Marvin: Did that piss you off?

Mr. Wilson: Hell yes, I just wanted to get this picture taken and get the fuck out of there.

Marvin: Did Tommy return with the tools?

Mr. Wilson: Yeah, well a tool, a pry bar. He started going to town on these wooden blocks on the floor holding the doors in place. The entire time, Becky is fucking talking to him. Every time I say something, she makes a snide remark towards me. Every fucking thing was going wrong! I can't get in the damn iron maiden, Becky is trying to get with Tommy, and there is no way I am gonna win that contest without that damn picture.

Marvin: Seems like you were having a bad night.

Mr. Wilson: I was.

Marvin: Did Tommy get the doors free?

Mr. Wilson: Finally, he pulled the doors open. I took a look inside, and it really had all these sharp things in it. I mean I thought they would remove them for safety or something like that.

Marvin: Did you get in the coffin like box with very sharp spikes on the inside?

Mr. Wilson: I didn't want to. Tommy said he would use the blocks to keep the doors open, so it would be safe. I was gonna say no. Then Becky started calling me a "little dicked wanna be." With "no balls." Fuck her, I went for it.

Marvin: You got in the iron maiden because of Becky?

Mr. Wilson: No man not because of her, that was my chance, I was gonna win, get on stage with the Iron Maiden. My life was about to take off.

Marvin: How did getting inside the iron maiden go?

Mr. Wilson: The getting it was easy, I opened the doors. Stepped inside. Not closing the doors was a little trickier.

Marvin: How so?

Mr. Wilson: I had to grab onto a couple of spikes on the inside of the door while Tommy gently closed the door. Then I held it open so I wouldn't get stabbed while Tommy stuck the block between the door and the frame. Then we had to do it again for the other door.

Marvin: Were you scared?

Mr. Wilson: Hell yeah, I was scared, those doors were heavy and the spikes were sharp. I could barely hold the doors open. I didn't notice when I got in but the iron maiden was tilted back just enough to weigh the doors in.

Marvin: Did the blocks work?

Mr. Wilson: Yeah, they worked. Tommy said you couldn't see them from the outside, but you could see my face. It was gonna be a bitching picture. I told Tommy to get the camera and take the picture, and you know what he said, "Where's the camera?" He didn't bring the nice camera. Fuck me, I started cussing. Then he had the balls to say he "would just use his phone, because it really didn't matter."

Marvin: How did you react?

Mr. Wilson: I started cussing him, told him I was gonna "kick his ass" when I got out. Then Becky started in on me and told Tommy he should take "her from behind." Yelling and more yelling. It sucked. I was yelling. Becky was yelling. Tommy was just standing there.

Marvin: What stopped the yelling?

Mr. Wilson: Tommy just said okay. He started walking behind Becky, unbuckling his pants. I could fucking see everything.

Marvin: What did you do?

Document I5 Interview: 78987654-8a

Mr. Wilson: I yelled, and I started pushing on the doors trying to get them open. But I just wasn't strong enough.

Marvin: Did it get worse?

Mr. Wilson: Yeah, he walked behind her and dropped his pants. He just walked up, took her and I could see her fucking face. She was enjoying it, fucking bitch.

Marvin: Were you still trying to get out of the iron maiden?

Mr. Wilson: I was trying but I just didn't have the strength, then I could hear the smacking of Tommy going into Becky. She was moaning and he was going to town. That pissed me off, I gave it one last push. Then I heard the sound.

Marvin: What sound?

Mr. Wilson: The block that was holding the door open dropped. I realized I didn't have enough muscle to actually open the heavy door. Then Pain.

Marvin: Do you remember anything else?

Mr. Wilson: The last thing I remember is the look of ecstasy on Becky's face.

Damnation recommendation:

Recommend Mr. Wilson be sent to the medieval torture section, in addition while he is in the torture devices "Candy Pop" music be played on a constant cycle. Damnation review in twelve-hundred-fifty years.

DOCUMENT 16

INTERVIEW: 78976552-9P

Interview: 78976552-9p

Demon: Pete-09864679-78*e4

<u>Soul</u>

Given Name: Terry Lane Horowitz

Also Known as: none

Occupation: Security Guard

Transcribed by: Demon Transcriber #09079878767653457a3b

Transcript

Pete-09864679-78*e4 (From here on referred to as "Pete".): It is my job to interview you to determine your damnation status and/or clarification of specifics of your level of damnation in Hell.

Terry Lane Horowitz (From here on referred to as "Mr. Horowitz".): What the fuck is going on?

Pete: I just explained it to you. Did you not understand what I said?

Mr. Horowitz: I think maybe I understand.

Pete: State your full name.

Mr. Horowitz: Terry Lane Horowitz.

Pete: Now what do you remember?

Mr. Horowitz: Wait, some fucker dragged me down a road.

Pete: Yes, you seem to not want to come to our little abode, some demons decide to speed you along.

Mr. Horowitz: I don't have time for this bullshit, I have places to be and people to see.

(Pete reaches and a file appears.)

Pete: According to the records you have no appointments scheduled, you have alienated everyone around you, so they avoid you. Let me see about your love life…

(Pete turns the page.)

Pete: …Your love life consists of…wait let me see. Oh yes, you have a premium subscription to the web site Pornhub, and occasionally you go on Onlyfans.

Mr. Horowitz: That's not true. I have a lot of girlfriends.

(Pete stands up, begins walking around the table and Mr. Horowitz.)

Pete: Some of the demons like to get elaborate on their motivation to the damned souls. They create all kinds of specialized tortures slowly torturing the soul. Now I must say that this can be effective for some of the damned. Myself, I have found that some of the damned just are not intelligent enough to understand the nuances of those elaborate torture routines. That all that specialized effort is just a waste.

Mr. Horowitz: Oh, thank god, torture would be horrible.

Pete: I guess I am old fashion. I prefer the old fashion beating, biting, and ripping apart.

(Pete begins to physically beat, bite, and rip Mr. Horowitz apart. The damaged parts grow back just fast enough that Pete can repeat the beating, biting, and ripping.)

Interview is delayed for six months four days while Pete performs old fashion motivation.

(Pete walks back, takes a seat. He reaches out and a large Sonic cup appears in his hand.)

Pete: Nothing like a Route 44 cherry lime-aide after a little work out, wouldn't you agree?

(Pete drinks while Mr. Horowitz' parts are slowly assembled back to his seat.)

Mr. Horowitz: I ah...I ah…I never really like them.

Pete: Well, there is no accounting for taste. Now back to your sex life, or the lack there of. I would suggest that you avoid lying. I really don't have the inclination or patience to deal with you or your mistruths, on the other hand I could stand a little more work out.

(Pete pops his knuckles in the style of a fighter.)

Mr. Horowitz: I have no sex life. I have not been with a woman since I was seventeen.

Pete: Was that sexual episode mutually voluntary?

Mr. Horowitz: She wanted…

(Pete's prehensile tail stabs through the side of Mr. Horowitz' jaw then changes direction and goes through the chest.)

Pete: Do not lie, do not tell half-truths. If you continue to try to do this, I will take steps to motivate you to cooperate.

(Pete's tail pulls out ripping parts of Mr. Horowitz as it comes out. The healing takes a few minutes.)

Mr. Horowitz: I forced her.

Pete: What is the name for that?

Mr. Horowitz: Rape, I raped her.

Pete: For your information, she liked you and most likely would have been willing on the next date. But because of what you did she killed herself six months later. That episode is one of the reasons you are damned. Not the only one, but one that we take special notice of. But that is not the reason I am here. I am more concerned with the night you died.

Mr. Horowitz: Then why did you bring it up?

Pete: Did it cause you pain to know that you have not had sex in seventeen years and that the last time you had to rape someone?

Mr. Horowitz: Yeah it hurts to say it.

Pete: Exactly, that is why. Now about the night you died. What do you remember?

Mr. Horowitz: I had worked all day at the warehouse, I am a security guard there, in fact I am the only security guard there.

Pete: By worked what did you actually mean?

Mr. Horowitz: I locked all the doors, looked at porn on my phone, masturbated, drank a half of a fifth of scotch and passed out in the back room.

Pete: Yes, you slept all day, until you were relieved by the next shift at midnight. Was this what you normally did at your security job?

Mr. Horowitz: Yeah pretty much that was my routine.

Pete: Such a conscientious employee. What did you do after you left work?

Mr. Horowitz: There was a little bar called Rowdys I wanted to go to. I was banned for a few years, but they said I could try again. I wanted to see what was happening there.

Pete: Is that the only reason you wanted to go there?

Mr. Horowitz: Okay, I wanted to figure out a way to make a big mess, just to say fuck you to the bar owner, Rowdy.

Pete: The owner that lifted the ban on you?

Mr. Horowitz: He was the same fucker that banned me in the first place, just for flirting with a girl.

Pete: By flirting, you mean harassing a bachelorette until the entire bachelorette party left taking a significant amount of money out of the owner's pocket.

Mr. Horowitz: Well, when you put it that way, I guess he had reasons to ban me.

Pete: Yes, he did, but he decided to give you another chance. You went there with the intent of doing something. What happened that night?

Mr. Horowitz: I headed to the bar straight from work. I parked my car and went in.

Pete: Had you sobered up from the day drinking?

Mr. Horowitz: Not really but I can drive with a buzz really good.

Pete: I am sure that no one would agree with you. What did you see when you went in?

Mr. Horowitz: It was kind of empty, guess that is what it is after midnight on a weeknight. As I walked through, I saw a guy sitting at a table with four beers.

Pete: Why did you notice that?

Mr. Horowitz: 'Cause the old bartender used to tell me I could only have two at closing time, something about the state law. She would always tell me I could only have two at a time, no more.

Pete: The bar was letting him break the law?

Mr. Horowitz: I guess. I went to the bar and ordered a beer. I put my $3.25 on the bar and the new bartender said it's $4.25. I told her that was ALL I was gonna pay. She took my beer before I even had a sip.

Pete: You put your $3.25 on the bar and it was not enough currency, and the bartender took your beer. Why didn't you just pay the extra dollar? Were you not going to give a tip?

Mr. Horowitz: Hell no, I wasn't gonna give a tip!

Pete: I am sure some of the demons who have visited up there and worked for tips will want to have a talk with you about that once this interview is completed. But why didn't you just pay the extra dollar?

Mr. Horowitz: That was my bosses' fault; he wouldn't give me an advance on my next week's paycheck. He gave an advance to Charlie when his brother died.

Pete: You are correlating your need of drinking money to Charlie needing money when his brother died?

Mr. Horowitz: Why not?

(Pete placed his face in his palm for several seconds.)

Pete: Just go on with your story.

Mr. Horowitz: I only had $3.25. I was kind of screwed, I needed to do something.

Pete: What did you do?

Mr. Horowitz: I turned around and saw the guy with four beers sitting on his table. He had barely touched the first one. He was just sitting there looking at the four beers.

Pete: This gave you an idea?

Mr. Horowitz: Hell yeah, it did. Why the fuck were they letting this guy break the law and she wouldn't even let me slide on a dollar.

Pete: What did you do?

Mr. Horowitz: I just walked up to his table, grabbed a beer and started drinking it.

Pete: Did he react?

Mr. Horowitz: He just looked at me for a minute, then…

Pete: Then what?

Mr. Horowitz: Well he was a lot bigger than I thought, he must have been hunched over or something. He grabbed me by the throat. I mean I couldn't feel the floor under my feet. He is just holding me there in the air with one hand.

Pete: Did he say anything?

Mr. Horowitz: Yeah, he started saying "fifteen years, fifteen fucking years…"

Pete: Is that all he did?

Mr. Horowitz: No, he started punching me and repeating "fifteen years." He would hit me, and then say, "fifteen years."

Pete: Is that all?

Mr. Horowitz: Do I have to talk about this?

Pete: I can always motivate you. I suggest you keep talking.

Mr. Horowitz: Then he must have really gotten pissed. He said "Motherfucker do you know what happened fifteen years ago today?" Then he punched me. God he could throw a punch, I felt my jaw crack.

Pete: Is that all?

Mr. Horowitz: No, he started telling me about Afghanistan and fifteen years ago. He was crying and talking about his friend Sergeant Miller. He just kept hitting, crying and telling me about how he couldn't save him.

Pete: What else did he do?

Mr. Horowitz: Ten years, he started saying "Ten years today." He fucking started slamming me into the wall. Where did he get the strength? It was like I was a ragdoll, he just kept slamming me against the wall. Then he said "Ten years ago today, my love, my life, my Lisa died. Because of a drunk driver like you! I saw you come in you drunk bastard, I bet you drove here!"

Pete: Was that the end?

Mr. Horowitz: You would think that he would have worn out. But no, he started saying "Five years, five fucking years ago." Then he began to squeeze my throat, where did he get his strength? I could barely breathe.

Pete: He was saying five years ago, did he say what happened five years ago?

Mr. Horowitz: I was getting fuzzy by this time, but I do remember him saying "Five years ago today, my little Maggie, my faithful dog died." He said something else, but I don't remember what it was until I was on the floor. He was standing over me, and was saying "Fifteen years ago, ten years ago, five years ago" he just stood there repeating it.

Pete: Is that the end of your memory?

Mr. Horowitz: No, I remember him saying one more thing.

Pete: What did he say?

Mr. Horowitz: He said, "Fifteen years ago had a bad day, ten years ago had a bad day, five years ago had a bad day and today I go to jail for killing a piece of trash."

Afternote:

The man that beat Mr. Horowitz to death was not convicted. Ten people came forward and testified that Mr. Horowitz attacked him and gave him no choice. Fifteen more were willing to testify the same thing. For the record, on the day fifteen years before he was in combat in Afghanistan and lost his friend to combat related injuries. On the day ten years before, his wife was hit by a drunk driver. On the day five years before his dog that helped him get through the death of his wife died of cancer. He had not let anyone or anything close to him from that day. On a related note, the bartender took an interest in him during the court case; they have been happily dating since he was acquitted.

Damnation recommendation:

Recommend the standard damnation for rape, Pig Rape Arena. Damnation review in ten-thousand years.

Damnation adjustment:

After several thousand demons asked to have some time to torture Mr. Horowitz. A thousand-year rotation on demon requested specialized torture was added after the standard rape damnation before review.

Interview: 9867054-5r

Demon: Tim-766518654*e4

<u>Soul</u>

Given Name: Kyle Larry Jones

Also Known as: Jonesy

Occupation: amateur Cook

Transcribed by: Demon Transcriber #09079878767653457a3b

Transcript

Tim-766518654*e4 (From here on referred to as "Tim".): It is my job to interview you to determine your damnation status and/or clarification of specifics of your level of damnation in Hell.

Kyle Larry Jones: (From here on referred to as "Mr. Jones".) Whadda you mean damnation?

Tim: Please state your name.

Mr. Jones: Not until you tell me what the fuck you mean my damnation?

Tim: Are you sure you do not wish to comply?

Mr. Jones: Fuck this place, fuck your mother, and fuck your sister and especially fuck you!

(Mr. Jones accompanies this with several rude gestures.)

Tim: I guess I should take that as a request.

(Tim reaches out and a phone appears in his hand and begins talking into the phone.)

Tim: Hello, yes this is Tim-766518654*e4....yes…I am calling because my current interviewee has made a specific request in regard to mother, and possibly one of my sisters. Yes, I see, ok I am sure that would be appropriate. Thank you, goodbye.

(Tim hangs up the phone.)

Tim: My mother, the mother of all demons is currently busy, but at least one of my sisters should be available.

Mr. Jones: What the fuck are you talking about?

(A large door appears on the side of the room, it opens to a tall, obviously female demon carrying a cat-o-nine tails in one hand with bamboo cane strapped at her waist.)

Tim: I would like to introduce you to my sister, Becky-0976754689-*5, she works in the corporal punishment division, her specialty is, well, corporal punishment. She is here to fulfill your request.

Mr. Jones: What the…

(The cat-o-nine tails moves fast to wrap around Mr. Jones' mouth, neck and wrists pulling him to the ground.)

Becky-0976754689-*5 (From here on referred to as "Becky".): Hello Tim, what was the request?

Tim: Hello Becky.

(Tim waves his hand, Mr. Jones voice comes from the air "Fuck this place, fuck you mother, and fuck your sister and especially fuck you!")

Becky: Oh, I am going have some fun with him.

Tim: Thank you for being available, just drop him off once you have finished.

Becky: No Tim, thank you.

(Becky smiling drags Mr. Jones through the open door.)

Tim: Well looks like I have some time to kill.

(A television appears on the wall and Tim starts flipping the channels. A phone appears on the table, rings, Tim picks it up.)

Tim: Hello. Oh, hello Mother, yes the soul made a request… Becky-0976754689-*5 has him at the moment…I am sure she would not mind you dropping by. Yes, I will wait… thank you mother, goodbye.

(Tim resumes watching television.)

Interview stopped for one-hundred and eighty-four years, two months, three days.

(Tim is sitting in a recliner, watching television, Becky comes in the door, pulling on a leash, Mr. Jones' head, that looks like it has been chewed from his body, is attached to the leash.)

Becky: Well that was enjoyable, my new puppy kind of got carried away on the body.

Tim: No, problem it' is always good for puppies to chew on things. I heard you had a visitor.

Becky: Yes, Mother stopped by and spent a few decades on some modern torture techniques. I learned a lot about waterboarding, and the proper way to remove limbs.

Tim: It is always good to learn from a master. I think I should resume the interview; you can just drop the head on the floor.

(Mr. Jones head hits the floor.)

Becky: Enjoy the interview.

(Becky walks out the door, and it vanishes. Tim waves. Mr. Jones' head begins to grow a body, lifts and moves to the chair.)

Tim: Now that we have fulfilled your request, state your full name.

Mr. Jones: I ah...I ah…what…ah…

Tim: Are you trying to make another request or are you going to state your name?

(Mr. Jones looks stricken with fear for a few moments.)

Mr. Jones: No request, no request.

Tim: Then state your full name.

Mr. Jones: Kyle Larry Jones… Kyle Larry Jones… Kyle Larry Jones

Tim: Mr. Jones we are here to get some information on your last day on earth, the day you died. Do you remember that day?

Mr. Jones: I ah..I ah…

Tim: Mr. Jones there are only two ways this interview is going to go, you answer my questions clearly and to the best of your memory, or I motivate you, which in this case I will just make a request to my sisters because I need to binge watch some television shows.

Mr. Jones: I will answer.

Tim: See how simple this is. Now do you remember the night you died?

Mr. Jones: I think I do. It is a little fuzzy.

Tim: Tell me about that day.

Mr. Jones: I was fighting with my girlfriend, Elise.

Tim: What were you fighting about?

Mr. Jones: She had taken me out to dinner the night before, some kind of expensive Japanese restaurant. She was pissed because I had told her it was a waste of money. I mean they didn't even cook the food.

Tim: I take it you had Sushi.

Mr. Jones: Yeah, we had Sushi, but it was all different. I thought Sushi was just those things wrapped in seaweed. But some of this was just pieces of raw fish. I mean how hard is it to just cut a piece and put it on the plate.

Tim: Did this fight escalate?

Mr. Jones: You could say that. She threw a bottle of vodka at me and walked out the door.

Tim: I take it she was very upset, what made her so upset?

Mr. Jones: Well, it was some things I said, she spent over a hundred dollars on the food, and most of it was not even cooked. She said it was hard to do it. I told her she was full of shit and that anyone could do it.

Tim: After she walked, out what did you do?

Mr. Jones: I had some beers and watched some TV. I wanted to give her some time to cool off and come back.

Tim: Did she come back?

Mr. Jones: Nope, normally she comes back after an hour or so. It was like five hours and nothing. I knew I had hit a nerve with her, but I knew I was right too.

Document I7 Interview: 9867054-5r

Tim: You knew you were correct? This part was important to you.

Mr. Jones: Hell yeah! You cannot let a woman prove you wrong. That is like basic being a man.

Tim: You could not let her prove you wrong, what did you do.

Mr. Jones: I called her, and talked really nice, but she was still pissed. That is when I came up with a brilliant idea.

Tim: What was your idea?

Mr. Jones: I would cook a Japanese meal for her, with all the sushi and shit.

Tim: Were you good at cooking?

Mr. Jones: I can follow the directions on a box. How hard could it be?

Tim: For the record, you have no training as a chef, and you do not cook regularly?

Mr. Jones: Why should I, that is what Elise is for.

(Tim sits staring blankly at Mr. Jones for a few moments.)

Tim: Continue with your memories.

Mr. Jones: I called Elise up and talked her into coming back that night. I told her I would prove how easy it was, that I would have a full meal of Sushi that I made waiting on her.

Tim: Did you proceed to fix the meal?

Mr. Jones: Yeah, I jumped on google and downloaded several recipes, but there was not a lot to them mostly about rice, and how to cut the fish. Like I said anyone could do that.

Tim: Did you have the ingredients in your house?

Mr. Jones: No, I had to run to the Foodlion to grab it. The problem was I had to improvise on some of the ingredients.

Tim: Foodlion is a grocery store?

Mr. Jones: Yeah, but they didn't seem to have the stuff I needed.

Tim: You had to improvise, but you had never fixed this before. Was that a problem?

Mr. Jones: It was no problem. I am a quick study. I found this sushi rolling bamboo mat to help me put it all together. Anyway, I headed back to my house and got to work.

Tim: How did the food preparation go?

Mr. Jones: Not as well as I hoped. I started cutting everything up, which was going ok. I mean it's just cutting it up. It may not have been as small as the stuff we had in the restaurant, but it was good enough.

Tim: Seems like you had everything under control. Did things start to go wrong?

Mr. Jones: Yeah when I tried to cook the rice, I burnt it a few times.

Tim: What do you mean a few times?

Mr. Jones: I burnt the rice six times, who would have thought making rice would be so hard. Anyway, I got it, it was a little crunchy, but I didn't burn it on the seventh time.

Tim: Just a little crunchy, how was everything else?

Mr. Jones: It was ok, I mean I lost a lot of time on the rice, but Elise wasn't supposed to be there until nine that night. I got everything put together and had time to clean an area to serve her on the table before Elise arrived.

Tim: How did the meal go?

Mr. Jones: Not well, I guess it takes some practice to wrap the seaweed, so it looks pretty like she wanted.

Tim: It was a little sloppy on the wraps? What about the Sashimi?

Mr. Jones: What do you mean, Sa…sa…sho…

Tim: The Sashimi, the fish served alone or on a bed of rice.

Mr. Jones: Not well at all, she got a little upset about some of my substitutions.

Tim: What kind of substitutions?

Mr. Jones: I guess I got the wrong kind of rice it was supposed to be a sticky rice.

Tim: She got upset about the rice?

Mr. Jones: She told me it was not cooked right, but that it would be ok. Then the veggies annoyed her, I guess I should not have substituted a potato for jicama, and I also decided to add some broccoli and mushrooms…I thought she would like it, she likes to order them when we go to dinner.

Tim: So it was the vegetables that got her really upset?

Mr. Jones: No, she was like it was an odd choice but that did not upset her the most. It was the fish.

Tim: How did the fish upset her?

Mr. Jones: Well I didn't know you were supposed to only use salt-water fish, I couldn't find any of the fish on the list that were already unfrozen. I decided to use some bluegill.

Tim: Bluegill, why Bluegill?

Mr. Jones: Well my friend had a bunch that he had caught, and I thought why use my money when he was willing to just let me have it.

Tim: It was the Bluegill that upset her?

Mr. Jones: Yeah, she was upset; she started yelling about tapeworms, lung flukes, and roundworms. I thought she wanted to eat raw fish. After a while, I got her to calm down. She asked me if I had any more Bluegill to poison her with. I told her I didn't have any more Bluegill. I mean why was she upset about Bluegill? We have eaten it many times before.

Tim: I am sure there was a reason. Was that the end of the night?

Mr. Jones: No, I had one more plate of food. I was getting pissed, I had spent a lot of money on this Japanese food for her. I worked hard to fix it and she was gonna eat some of it. She had not eaten one mouthful yet.

Tim: What was left?

Mr. Jones: What did you call it, the Sosumo?

Tim: The Sashimi.

Mr. Jones: Yeah that stuff. I was tired of her remarks; she was acting so smart. I knew my food didn't look as good as the Japanese place. But I knew how to show her my food was good. I got her to close her eyes as I came in carrying the Sosumi.

Tim: The Sashimi, how did that work out?

___

Mr. Jones: Sashimi, yeah. I took some of it, and put it in her mouth, her eyes closed…

Tim: What happened?

Mr. Jones: She threw up all over the floor… and started screaming at me. She said I tried to kill her, and how much of an idiot I am. Then grabbed a bottle of water and ran out of the house while trying to wash her mouth out.

Tim: Why was she calling you an idiot?

Mr. Jones: Well like I said the Foodlion didn't have the fish unfrozen that the recipes called for. I had to do a little substitution…I had made her chicken Sashimi.

Tim: Wait, what?

Mr. Jones: I made chicken Sashimi.

Tim: You made chicken Sashimi?

Mr. Jones: Yeah, I mean we eat chicken all the time. I didn't see what the issue was.

Tim: Chicken Sashimi…you made chicken Sashimi.

Mr. Jones: I don't know what the issue was, after she left, and I cleaned up the mess she made I drank a few beers and ate the leftovers. They seemed ok to me.

Tim: Do you remember anything after you went to bed that night?

Mr. Jones: I had to get up and use the bathroom, my stomach seemed a little upset.

Tim: The reason you do not remember anything is you died from salmonella and campylobacter poisoning. You took three days to die in your bed. Elise would have saved you but the food you put in her mouth gave her salmonella poisoning and she was in the hospital, but she recovered.

Damnation Recommendation:

Recommend Mr. Jones is put in the chicken farm as feed. His hunger should be drastically increased. Restrictions on what he can eat should be restricted to chicken poop. Damnation review in fifteen-hundred years.

DOCUMENT 18

INTERVIEW: 9875678-989755

Interview: 9875678-989755

Demon: Lisa-09878658-08*e4

<u>Soul</u>

Given Name: John Montoya Williams

Also Known as: none

Occupation: Fitness Coach, Television personality, Murderer

Transcribed by: Demon Transcriber #0907987876765-3457a3b

Transcript

Lisa-09878658-08*e4 (From here on referred to as "Lisa".): It is my job to interview you to determine your damnation status and/or clarification of specifics of your level of damnation in Hell.

John Montoya Williams: (From here on referred to as "Mr. Williams ".): Wait, what, where am I?

Lisa: I will say it again. It is my job to interview you to determine your damnation status and/or clarification of specifics of your level of damnation in Hell. Now please state your full name.

Mr. Williams: James Montoya Williams, I'm Jim from Jim's Fitness Show we're number one in the tri-state area.

Lisa: Do you understand where you are?

Mr. Williams: I think I do, Charon the Riverman told me, and some guy got fed to a three headed dog. Kind of made the point. Can I ask you a question? Do you need a fitness coach to get in shape? I mean with the way you are built I could make you so fit.

(Lisa looked up at Mr. Williams. The look of boredom that was on her face gave way to the fire that filled her eyes and a smile showing sharp teeth stretched across her face.)

Lisa: Mr. Williams are you in the habit of implying that the people around you are out of shape?

Mr. Williams: Well to be honest most are out of shape like you.

Lisa: Please enlighten me as to how you think I am out of shape?

Mr. Williams: Well, just look at you. That suit you wear does nothing but hide your flabby body, you sit all wrong like the muscles in your back are weak… and don't get me started on that fat around your horns…wait horns.

Lisa: Go on.

Mr. Williams: Your tail is…wait tail?

Lisa: Mr. Williams, I do not think you understand your predicament. You are in Hell, that is the capital H, Hell. Your entire life has been to tear down other people. Now you will say things like that you tear them down to build them back up. You have never built anyone up but yourself. You are a weak-minded little man with little dick syndrome.

(Lisa reaches out and rips off the pants and underwear exposing his genitals.)

Lisa: See I knew it, a true micro dick.

(Mr. Williams runs at Lisa in an attempt to attack, Lisa reaches out and easily catches him. One twist of his wrist Mr. Williams screams in pain.)

Lisa: Now about your offer of a fitness coach to get in shape.

(Lisa's clothes dissolve and a workout outfit takes their place. She has muscles all over her body, she is in great shape.)

Lisa: I do not need a coach. But what I do need is some fitness equipment. I have been so busy I have been unable to catch a good workout. But there is no time like the present.

(A chain comes out of the wall and begins to wrap around Mr. Williams. The chain reaches up and pulls Mr. Williams into a position imitating a heavy bag. The song "Eye of the Tiger" begins playing in the background.)

Lisa: You know there is nothing like a good heavy bag workout to begin with, especially when you have to deal with micro dicked pussies all day.

(Lisa begins to do a heavy bag workout in time with the music, pounding Mr. Williams into pulp.)

Lisa: Now that is a nice little workout. You know I should get in a full workout.

(During the next seven years and five days, Lisa works out on various heavy bag routines.)

Lisa: That is enough of the heavy bag, now for the speed bag.

(The chains pull Mr. Williams until he is upside down with his head in the position of the speed bag. Lisa does the speed bag routine for six years, four months, five days.)

Lisa: Wow, nothing like a workout to take away the stress of the day.

(Lisa walks back towards her desk. A shower stall appears with frosted glass. She walked in one side, out the other. The sweat and workout clothes are replaced with the business suit. Mr. Williams is pulled and pushed by the chains into the interview chair.)

Lisa: Now that I have worked off a little stress, we shall continue the interview. Mr. Williams we are here to clarify some issues so that your damnation is as effective as possible. Do you remember your last day alive?

Document I8 Interview: 9875678-989755

Mr. Williams: I…I…I remember it yes, I remember it.

Lisa: Tell me about it.

Mr. Williams: I was at my gym when I was told I had a phone call. I hate taking phone calls. It's always bad news.

Lisa: Was it bad news?

Mr. Williams: Yeah, it was really bad news.

Lisa: What was the news?

Mr. Williams: A few years ago, I came up with this idea of a major weight loss campaign to boost my gym's membership. You know we find some fatty, take some pictures really showing how bad they look. Force them to work out for a few months, then take new shots making them look good. Hell, half the time we took the before and after photos the same day and just fudged the numbers. It's amazing what you can do with clear tape and a little creativity.

Lisa: You mean you ran a scam to make your gym look like it was good at helping people lose weight?

Mr. Williams: I guess that you could say it that way, but I called it a campaign. But the funny thing is it worked, my gym business took off, and I got a show. That Little campaign set me up. The last five years had been going well until…

Document I8 Interview: 9875678-989755

Lisa: Until?

Mr. Williams: Until about six months ago, I got a call from a reporter. It seems she was trying to find the "people" we helped to do a follow up. I knew that she was gonna find out how we "fudged" the numbers to make us look good.

Lisa: Is that all that happened?

Mr. Williams: That's not enough? But no that was not all. We had a total of ten "clients" that we used for the campaign. I got calls from five of them just asking for money to shut up. Three of them had had gastric bypass surgery so they were a lot smaller.

Lisa: What about the other two?

Mr. Williams: They were no problem. They both had died.

Lisa: How did they die? Now before you answer remember we have a full record of your life. Up to and including how you got a "C" in your high school chemistry class. Mr. Charles Johnson, your teacher, was very happy with your demonstration of fellatio.

Mr. Williams: You know about that?

Lisa: Mr. Williams we know all, I can make a list if you want. But most of them are not even worth mentioning. Now how did the other two die?

Mr. Williams: I killed them.

Lisa: How did you kill them?

Mr. Williams: I invited them to my gym, gave them some candy laced with an extreme workout drug. It's ok in small doses if you are in shape. With the fact that they had trouble walking upstairs, it didn't take much. One of them didn't make it home, he must have eaten the candy in his car. The other died in bed with her husband. He thought he had killed her. Both deaths were ruled a heart attack.

Lisa: What happened to her husband?

Mr. Williams: He committed suicide the next month.

Lisa: Why did you kill them?

Mr. Williams: They said they were going to go to the press with the campaign information. I would have lost my show, and maybe my gym. I had no choice.

Lisa: Humans always have a choice; you made the wrong choice. Now about this call you received. Why was it bad news?

Mr. Williams: The campaign, I had forgotten we actually had eleven not ten. We had an extra in case something happened. The extra was talking to the reporter. Even though she was never actually in the campaign she could know enough to damage me.

Lisa: You had forgotten about number eleven. What did you do?

Document I8 Interview: 9875678-989755

Mr. Williams: I went to my office and got the information on the extra. I kept all the records, and I was hoping that I could talk some sense into her or bribe her.

Lisa: Did either of those work?

Mr. Williams: When I got her information, I knew that both would fail.

Lisa: Why, who was she?

Mr. Williams: Her name was La'ei Burgess. Which when you think of it is kind of an odd name. The reason we could not use her in the campaign was she was Samoan, and honestly was just a six-foot-four, three-hundred-fifty-pound woman made of muscle. She was stronger than the male trainers and very athletic. I didn't meet her until later in the campaign. I let someone else recruit for the campaign, in fact the shoots were almost over by the time I actually met her. I had seen her name, but I didn't realize that was her married name.

Lisa: Why would you not use her? With her height and weight, it doesn't seem too difficult to make it look like you helped her.

Mr. Williams: She was a monster. She was throwing weights around like they were fake. While we were shooting one loser, the shot was totally ruined because she was doing the standing crate jump in the background. She wouldn't let us "tape her up" to make her look less fat for the "after" shots.

It was a nightmare. But the last straw was when one of our workout Gurus slipped and "accidentally" grabbed her breast.

Lisa: Did she react?

Mr. Williams: She put him into a brick wall, he spent a week in the hospital. She walked out. I had to get a biohazard team to come in and clean up all the blood.

Lisa: This La'ei was the bad news, you could not talk to her and you could not bribe her. What did you come up with?

Mr. Williams: My first thought was the special candy I gave the other two. But I dismissed that, it didn't really seem like I could get her to eat it. I gave it some thought.

Lisa: What did you come up with?

Mr. Williams: I decided I had to do it the old fashion way. I had her address from the forms she filled out when she applied for the campaign. If luck was on my side, she would still live in the same location.

Lisa: You decided to go and see if you could kill her.

Mr. Williams: It seemed like the easiest thing. I could make it look like a botched robbery or something. Just go in kill her, mess up the place. Hell, I might even burn it down to hide everything.

Document I8 Interview: 9875678-989755

Lisa: Seems like you had a plan. Tell me about that night.

Mr. Williams: Luck seemed to be on my side. Her house was down a little way from a bike trail that was popular in the area. I tossed my mountain bike on my car and headed out.

Lisa: Any luck when you got there?

Mr. Williams: Nothing but luck. I stopped close to her address, massaging my leg like I had a cramp. There she was standing on the porch in some flowing flower dress. Nothing had changed. She was just as big as the last time I saw her. There was a guy standing on the porch in front of her, he was as big as she was. He made me question my plan a little. I saw him kiss her, pick up a suitcase and walk to a blue SUV. This must be my lucky day. Her husband must have been leaving for a trip. Could my luck get any better?

Lisa: Lucky you.

Mr. Williams: Hell yell, lucky me, I followed the bike path around until I found a place that looked like the teenagers used to smoke pot. It was behind a bunch of scrub brush just above her house.

Lisa: Why did you do that?

Mr. Williams: I made the decision as soon as I saw her husband leave that I needed to do it then and there. It was almost dark enough I just had to wait about an hour. I spend an hour trying to get a better look at the back of her house. There was a privacy fence, but I was pretty sure I could get over that. I was just hoping that there were no dogs.

Lisa: You waited until dark? Then you struck?

Mr. Williams: Yeah, I struck, as soon as it was dark, I sprinted towards the fence. I went over it just like the parkour guys in France do. Bam I was over the fence and inside her yard. I stopped crouching while watching for a dog. Nothing, I started moving to the back of the house. My luck was holding, the back door was open, there was nothing but a little screen door with a hook lock holding it.

Lisa: Did that slow you down?

Mr. Williams: No way, I just put my hand though the screen and unlocked it. That is when I thought I was going to have a heart attack.

Lisa: What happened?

Mr. Williams: A dog, a fucking little ankle biting dog no bigger than my fucking hand. It started raising a racket.

Lisa: I don't think that you were afraid of the dog?

Mr. Williams: Hell no, but the bitch might alert the bitch…see what I did there.

(Lisa reached out and slapped Mr. Williams, spinning his head completely around.)

Lisa: DO NOT do that.

(Mr. Williams's head slowly returns to facing the correct way.)

Mr. Williams: It won't happen again.

Lisa: Good, now you were afraid of the little dog alerting your victim?

Mr. Williams: Yeah but turns out she thought the dog was wanting to chase birds or something. La'ei came around a corner talking to the dog. Saw me standing there. Too soon I didn't even have a weapon yet.

Lisa: How did you react?

Mr. Smith: I froze for a minute; she took off around the corner. But the freeze helped me, I was looking at this short blunt sword with a hook on the wall. I must have missed it before.

Lisa: Yes, that would be the Nifo-oti, it is a Samoan weapon.

Mr. Williams: Whatever it was, it was heavy, I had to use two hands just to hold it up. It would do the job. Now I just had to find her.

Lisa: Did you find her?

Mr. Williams: I went around the corner and there she was. She wasn't running, she was just standing in the middle of the kitchen. She took one look at me and said, "That was my father's you need to put it down now."

Lisa: How did you respond?

Mr. Williams: I said, "Fuck you bitch!" I raised the …sword and ran towards her. I thought she would run away, but she just yelled something and came at me.

Lisa: Did that go well for you?

Mr. Williams: I didn't realize she had something in her hands when I came in. It seemed to be some type of hooked club, with designs on it.

Lisa: Did you get her with the short sword?

Mr. Williams: I missed… I mean I missed. How do you miss a six-foot-four three-hundred-fifty-pound woman? She moved so fast, I swung, and she moved.

Lisa: Did she miss?

Mr. Williams: No, she did not miss.

Lisa: Where did she hit?

Mr. Williams: I went high with the sword in a big swing I missed. She went for the gut, with the wooden hook. She didn't miss.

Lisa: She gutted you with one hit?

Mr. Williams: Yes, I was looking down at my own guts.

Lisa: Is that the last thing you remember?

Mr. Williams: No, I was standing there, looking down at the insides of my stomach. Wondering what had happened, how I had missed. When I heard a yell behind me, and I saw the bloody wooden hook coming up from between my legs. Then darkness.

Afternote:

Mr. Williams was gutted by La'ei Burgess with a traditional Samoan War club that included a wooden hook. The war yell and hook coming between his legs was the last blow. It lifted him so hard that his head went into the ceiling, into the darkness.

Damnation recommendation:

Recommend Mr. Williams serves as under-used fitness equipment in a nursing home, fully conscious the entire time. Damnation review in seven-hundred years.

DOCUMENT 19

INTERVIEW: 9845678-87654

Interview: 9845678-87654

Demon: Milton-u935029-976*e4

<u>Soul</u>

Given Name: Nickolas Jackson Stump

Also Known as: Stumpy

Occupation: Dog Fight Trainer

Transcribed by Demon Transcriber #0907987876765-3457a3b

Transcript

Milton-u935029-976*e4 (From here on referred to as "Milton".): It is my job to interview you to determine your damnation status and/or clarification of specifics of your level of damnation in Hell.

Nickolas Jackson Stump: (From here on referred to as "Mr. Stump".): Ah…what?

Milton: I am here to determine some specifics, so the damnation process is efficient. Now please state your full name.

Mr. Stump: Nick, you can just call me Nick.

Milton: I said state your full name.

Mr. Stump: I said you can call me Nick.

Milton: You seem to be under the impression that you have some type of control, I think I can show you that you do not.

(Milton waves, heavy rubber tubes come out from the four corners of the room and grab Mr. Stump by the wrist and arms suspending him in the middle of the room.)

Mr. Stump: Look at this, what do you have some type of rubber fetish?

Milton: No, I do not have a rubber fetish. I have more of an electrical fetish. The rubber is there as an insulator. What I do have is an interest in the competition at the beginning of the 20th century between Alexander Graham Bell and Nikola Tesla. Are you familiar with the competition that was basically alternating current versus direct current? It is a fascinating part of the American persona. Two men competing using scientific discoveries, right in the public eye.

Mr. Stump: I have no clue what you are talking about.

Milton: That says a lot about the sad state of the education system. But alas I am not here to give you a history lesson.

Mr. Stump: Thank fucking god, you were boring the shit out of me.

Milton: You will find that boredom in Hell is seldom an issue. Now as you are suspended by rubber, you have no "ground" for electricity to go to. This actually prevents you from being shocked. Here let me demonstrate.

(A high voltage cable drops from the ceiling landing beside Mr. Stump's chest. Mr. Stump tries to pull away from the cable. Nothing happens.)

Mr. Stump: What the fuck, you could have killed me.

Milton: No for two reasons, first you are already dead. Second, you did not provide a path to ground for the electricity. On the other hand, if I was to say hook a cable to your big toe that goes to ground...

(A cable comes from the floor and attaches to Mr. Stump's right big toe. As soon as it touches sparks start flying from the cable in his chest. Mr. Stump shakes violently until the cable is pulled up to the ceiling. Smoke is rising from Mr. Stump's body.)

Milton: That was alternating current, notice how your body shook. Back and forth, muscles flexing involuntarily.

Mr. Stump: I ah…I ah…

Milton: No, I have to show you that you are not in control. Now where was I, oh yeah that was alternating current. This on the other hand is direct current.

(A second cable comes from the ceiling and touches Mr. Stump's chest. Mr. Stump's body goes rigid, like every muscle in his body is contracting. He stays like this until the cable is pulled away. Mr. Stump then hangs limply. Smoke is coming from his body.)

Milton: Did you see the difference? A totally different type of shock. Wouldn't you agree?

Mr. Stump: I ah…I ah…

Milton: Now I have read all about different things they did to test the different electrical shocks during the competition between Bell and Tesla. Did you know the Bell electrocuted an elephant to show how dangerous alternating current was? Wait you didn't know anything about it at all so never mind.

Mr. Stump: Elepha…

Milton: But you know what I could not find information on? Internal shocks, shocks to the inside of the body.

Mr. Stump: In…in... inside?

Milton: Yes, inside. I came up with a few ideas to try it out.

(A table appears with many devices on it. Most are metal, some are metal with rubber protections on parts. Milton reaches down and grabs a gold wire about twelve inches long with a small ball on each end.)

Mr. Stump: Inside…what do you mean inside?

Milton: This for example, I wonder how much voltage this wire can impart before it melts? Shall we find out.

(Mr. Stump's pants are ripped off. The wire floats from Milton's hand and inserts itself into the hole on the end of Mr. Stump's penis leaving about an inch of wire sticking out. The alternating current wire begins to come down to Mr. Stump's groin area.)

Milton: Now, let's see how this goes shall we.

Mr. Stump: No, no, no, no…

(The alternating current wire contacts the wire that is still sticking out. Mr. Stump screams.)

Milton: I almost forgot the music.

(Classical music starts coming from the surrounding walls.)

Milton: That is better.

(Milton continues to shock Mr. Stump internally, using different probes for the next ten years, five months and six days.)

Milton: Now that was very informative.

Mr. Stump: Thank god that is over.

Milton: The first half is over, now we must switch polarity and do all the shocks in the opposite direction.

Mr. Stump: Half…half…half over.

(The three cables retract. The ground cable then drops from the ceiling. The two other cables grow from the floor. Milton repeats all of the shocks using the reversed polarity. This takes another ten years, five months, and six days.)

Milton: That was informative.

(Mr. Stump is lowered into the chair, the rubber tubes retract into the walls.)

Milton: Now that you know you are NOT in control. State your full name.

Mr. Stump: Nickolas Jackson Stump… Nickolas Jackson Stump

Milton: Mr. Stump, this interview is just to determine some specifics on your damnation. We strive to be the best we can be. We know most things in your life. We mainly have questions about the last day you were alive. Do you remember that day?

Mr. Stump: Yes I remember, I had a big fight.

Milton: Big fight day? You are a fighter?

Mr. Stump: Kind of, I fight dogs.

(Milton reaches out and smacks Mr. Stump's head off, it rolls to the wall. Milton reaches and a file appears. Milton begins reading it. Milton reaches out, a phone appears and he begins talking into the phone.)

Milton: Hello this is Milton-u935029-976*e4, yes…no…I have one, oh yes one of those…no I did not review the file beforehand. Yes, I understand. No, I want to keep this one…oh yes please notify the puppy brigade. Thank you…have a good day.

(Milton reaches down and picks up Mr. Stump's head. Smashes it against the wall, then puts it back on the top of the body. It begins to heal.)

Milton: Seems I have made a little misstep. I did not review your file before I began the interview. As a result, I have not treated you appropriately.

Mr. Stump: What do you mean?

Milton: Hell is a bureaucracy, we have very specific rules on certain souls, and how they are to be treated.

Mr. Stump: You are saying I am supposed to get special treatment? That I am a special soul?

Milton: Yes, technically would be correct. You are to receive special treatment because you are a special soul.

Mr. Stump: I knew it; I knew there was something wrong.

Milton: Yes, I will be receiving a reprimand once this interview is over. I have been notified that I need to begin the special treatment as soon as possible.

Mr. Stump: Special treatment that is more like it.

(Milton waves a hand and a choke collar appears on Mr. Stump's neck. A chain begins pulling the choke collar up and back away from Mr. Stump.)

Mr. Stump: Wait, wait, you said I was to get special treatment.

Milton: You are, see I was being too nice to you. Dog fighters and anyone associated with them are a special treat for demons. We get a special bonus' for the treatment of any and all dog fighters.

(Mr. Stump's body withdrew to an emaciated frame, so he displayed a skeleton-like visage.)

Milton: We actually can get a few days off as a bonus for our creativity when it comes to dog fighting souls.

Mr. Stump: But why, they are just animals.

(Mange-like areas appear all over Mr. Stump's body. Straps appear holding his hands just far enough away from his body so that he cannot scratch.)

Milton: Did you ever wonder why dogs are so loyal? Why did they remain so faithful to you after you treated them so badly time and time again?

Mr. Stump: I thought they were just stupid.

(Demon enhanced fleas appear all over Mr. Stump's body and begin feasting on him.)

Milton: Dogs are part of heaven sent to be on earth. They were sent to earth to be a human's friend. You were mistreating a gift from heaven.

Mr. Stump: Sounds pretty stupid to me? Why the hell would a demon care about that?

Milton: I guess you had no education, the Great Adversary, which you know as Satan is a fallen angel. When he fell, before he landed in Hell, a dog, a mixed-up mutt, took a moment to lick his hand. Being exactly what dogs were meant to be, loyal and faithful. From that day forward anyone who mistreats dogs gets special attention in Hell. You will get special treatment for the rest of eternity.

(Two-inch worms with round toothy mouths appear on the ground and begin to crawl up Mr. Stump's legs, when they get to his anus, they begin to chew their way inside.)

Mr. Stump: But they were just dogs.

Milton: There is nothing as "just" dogs.

(The worms are now crawling under the skin in Mr. Stump's abdomen.)

Mr. Stump: …Just dogs.

Milton: I still have to interview you, so it will give me a chance to make up for my earlier mistake.

(A pair of metal bowls appear on the table, one with food and one with water. Mr. Stump attempts to get to them. The bowls are just an inch or two out of reach.)

Milton: Mr. Stump tell me about the last things you remember.

Mr. Stump: …I remember a fight was coming up. I had to get ready for it.

Milton: What did "get ready" for it consist of?

Mr. Stump: Killer, my best dog needed a work-out. I wanted him to get some more blood work, so I grabbed one of the bait dogs, and pulled it to the workout rings.

(The sound of dogs in the distance begins.)

Milton: What do you mean bait dogs?

Mr. Stump: They're dogs we use to train the fighters, any type will work.

(Dogs seem to be baying in the distance. Mr. Stump is looking around for where the sounds are coming from.)

Milton: Where do you get these dogs?

Mr. Stump: Anywhere we can. People getting rid of them, free pounds, hell I have grabbed them out of a yard as I went by.

(Baying dogs seem to be coming from a different direction. Mr. Stump is getting restless.)

Milton: Do you feed these dogs?

Mr. Stump: Why would I waste the money to feed bait dogs?

(A particularly vicious sound seems to come closer. Mr. Stump is starting to pull at the choke collar, it just gets tighter.)

Milton: You take any dog you can get your hands on, sometimes stealing them out of yards. Then use as bait to train the dogs to fight?

(Mr. Stump is looking around nervously.)

Milton: Is that correct?

Mr. Stump: Yeah pretty much.

Milton: You took your "bait" dog to the center of the ring. Why did it stay there?

Mr. Stump: We use a stake and tie the dog to it, we use a muzzle so it cannot fight back and hurt the other dog before the fight.

(A large thump hits the wall from the other side, a growl that sounds like it comes from a jaw that could chew car tires while the care is still moving comes through the wall.)

Mr. Stump: What is that?

Milton: The Puppy Brigade, don't worry they cannot get in.

Mr. Stump: Thank god...thank god.

Milton: You staked the dog in the middle, put a muzzle on it so it cannot fight back. Is that all correct?

Mr. Stump: Yeah, I had a winner in Killer, well actually it's like Killer forty-five, I always name them killer. Anyway Killer, was a killer. I was gonna bet everything on him. It was like a week away and I wanted him in top form.

Milton: Continue telling me about the day.

Mr. Stump: So anyway, the bait dog was in the middle of the ring. I just had to go get Killer. Wow he was gonna make me a bundle. I actually had to be careful around him because he wanted to take down anything, and everything. I grabbed him and took him to the outskirts of the ring. I was about to let him go when I saw the little shit bait dog had gotten out of his muzzle and had almost chewed through the strap that was holding him to the stake.

Milton: What did you do?

Mr. Stump: I didn't want to chase that little shit all over the place so I threw Killer's leash over a post and tied a quick knot. He was trying to go nuts. He was pulling the leash already. I went into the ring to grab the bait dog. That little shit got loose just as I got there. I grabbed it just in time.

Milton: You grabbed the little dog just as it was about to make its escape?

Mr. Stump: Yeah, I just got a hold of the part it chewed through. I drug it back to the center. I had to figure out how to get it tied. I was holding it there when I noticed that Killer wasn't barking.

Milton: Killer was not barking, what was he doing?

Mr. Stump: That bastard was working the knot I had put in his leash. As I looked, the knot came loose. I had left the door to the ring open in my haste to catch the bait dog. Killer came running, ready to attack. I knew I was fucked so I grabbed at the bait dog. My plan was to throw it at Killer and get the fuck out of that ring.

(The sounds of howling, scratching and growling are all round the room now. Large thumps keep hitting the wall shaking the room. Mr. Stump is looking from wall to wall.)

Milton: Did that work?

Mr. Stump: The fucking bait dog bit my hand; it started shaking it. I think it broke my hand.

Milton: What about Killer?

Mr. Stump: Just as the bait dog let go and ran like hell out of the ring, Killer came in.

(Howls came from outside, it continued for thirty to forty seconds.)

Milton: What did Killer do?

Mr. Stump: He did exactly what I had taught him to do…he attacked me, I couldn't stop him, he just went crazy. He ripped off my nuts…

Milton: Damn it, I almost forgot.

(Milton reaches out and violently removes Mr. Stumps groin area.)

Milton in Bob Barkers voice from the price is right: "This is Bob Barker reminding you to help control the pet population — have your pets spayed or neutered."

Milton: I always loved Bob Barker.

Mr. Stump: …Spayed? Wait spayed?

Milton: Do you remember anything else?

Mr. Stump: Just Killer standing over me with one of my nuts hanging from his mouth. He dropped it and went for my throat. I don't remember anything else.

Milton: Good, I really hate listening to people like you. Now the Puppy Brigade can have you.

Mr. Stump: But you said they couldn't get in.

Milton: They cannot.

(Milton reaches out, grabs Mr. Stump by the back of the neck, reaches for a door that appears and throws Mr. Stump to the Puppy Brigade.)

Afternote:

The bait dog was rescued, rehabilitated, adopted and loved by a family with a little girl. The bait dog happily guarded that little girl for the rest of its life.

Damnation Recommendation:

Recommend Mr. Stump be given to the Puppy Brigade per standard damnation for dog abusers. Starvation, mange, fleas, worms and spaying accomplished. Damnation Review recommended after five-thousand years for mistreatment of each dog.

DOCUMENT 20

INTERVIEW: 1234567-8760894

Interview: I234567-8760894

Demon: George-s7569-099094567*e4

Soul

Given Name: Lance Allen Donald

Also Known as: none

Occupation: Professional protester

Transcribed by: Demon Transcriber #09079878767653457a3b

Transcript

George-s7569-099094567*e4 (From here on referred to as "George".): It is my job to interview you to determine your damnation status and/or clarification of specifics of your level of damnation in Hell.

Jacob Edward Donald: (From here on referred to as "Mr. Donald".): It worked, holy shit it worked. We are here to show you, you fucking fascist.

George: Please state your full name.

Mr. Donald: I don't have to tell you shit. Down with the demons, up with the damned.

(George reaches out, grabs Mr. Donald by the testicles, and twists.)

George: If you don't tell me your full name, I am gonna twist until I hear them go pop.

Mr. McDonald: Lance Allen Donald… Lance Allen Donald… Lance Allen Donald

(There is an audible pop as George twists the testicles off.)

George: Oops, guess you should have been faster.

Mr. Donald: That's abuse, you and your demon friends have been abusing souls. We are here to stop you.

George: Mr. Donald do you realize you are dead, and that you are in Hell?

Mr. Donald: Of course, that was the plan.

George: The plan, you planned to be dead and in Hell?

Mr. Donald: Damn right we did. The truth has broken loose and we are here to put a stop to it. We are gonna protest until Hell changes.

George: You are gonna protest in Hell? Hold on I think I may need to check a few things.

(George reaches for a file that appears in his hand and begins reading.)

George: Mr. Donald, you are here to protest the mistreatment of damned souls, now that you are a damned soul?

Mr. Donald: That's right, it's time for change and we are here to make the changes.

George: Just a minute.

(A ball gag and straps appear on Mr. McDonald. George reaches for a phone that appears, begins talking into it.)

George: Yes this is George-s7569-099094567*e4…no, I may need a little guidance on Interview I234567-8760894. Yes I will wait…Yes that is correct. Okay I will wait for your supervisor…Hello, yes this is George-s7569-099094567*e4, yes interview I234567-8760894…Yes here to protest the treatment of damn souls…you can stop laughing any time now…ok I will wait for your supervisor…

(This waiting on supervisors, them laughing then transferring to their supervisor went on for two years, eleven months, and eight days, until George reached the correct level of a supervisor to advise him.)

Continuation of phone conversation

George: If you could just stop laughing long enough…yes Ma'am a complete idiot, I agree. But what…Yes I know. But Ma'am…Okay, I understand. Have a good day.

(George begins reading the file very closely, every so often he mumbles and cusses. After two days George looks up waves, the ball gag and straps release from Mr. McDonald.)

Mr. Donald: You just left me there tied to the chair, no food, no water what kind of a monster are you.

(George reaches out, grabs Mr. McDonald by the throat, lifts him and the chair up to the ceiling. George then points at himself.)

George: Demon.

Mr. Donald: Oh.

(George drops Mr. Donald. When he lands snaps a few bones.)

George: Now this is how this is going to work. You are going to tell me about your last day of life and answer any questions I have. If you do not, I will spend ten years torturing you until you decide that cooperation is the best choice.

Mr. Donald: But I am here to protest you, it's not fair.

George: I will take that as you are not going to cooperate, honestly I thought you didn't have the balls to volunteer for ten years of torture. Oh well have it your way.

Mr. Donald: Wait, wait, I didn't make a choice. I…

(A ball gag appears on Mr. Donald.)

George: Because you are here to protest the teaching techniques the demons are using on damned souls. I will only use the ones that humans developed. That should make you happy.

Document 20 Interview: I234567-8760894

(Mr. Donald shakes his head up and down. Under him a sharpened pole appears rising until it makes contact with Mr. Donald's anus. Then gently lifts him. Ropes appear holding Mr. McDonald on to the pole, but not pulling him down.)

George: Are you familiar with the person Count Dracula is named after? His name was Vlad Dracula, but more commonly known as Vlad the Impaler. He was just a human man. We will start with him. He impaled just under eighty thousand people. You will be impaled eighty thousand times one for each of the ones Dracula impaled. It may take more than ten years, but I want to get the point across.

(Mr. Donald is impaled eighty-thousand times, each time it takes three days. The impaling takes six-hundred-fifty-seven years.)

George: Now that we are warmed up, we can continue with some more human ideas.

(The ball gag disappears.)

Mr. Donald: You said ten years...that was like seven hundred years.

George: Don't exaggerate, that couldn't have been more than six hundred and eighty years. But we have so much more to explore. Have you heard of Elizabeth Báthory, she doesn't have Vlad's numbers but she has variety.

(Ball gag appears on Mr. Donald.)

George: After this we get into the heavy hitters, ever hear of Tomás de Torquemada? He was the first Grand Inquisitor in the Spanish Inquisition.

(George stands up and takes a pose with his hand on his hip.)

George in a English accent: Nobody expects the Spanish Inquisition.

George: Man, Those Monty Python Guys were funny.

(Mr. Donald is strapped to the table and torture devices appear around him. During the next seventeen hundred years, Mr. Donald is subject to some of the torture developed by humans.)

George: Now that you know how cruel humans can be, we should be able to continue the interview without difficulty from you.

(The ball gag disappears.)

Mr. Donald: I didn't know the Spanish Inquisition was real…oh god it was real.

George: Are you ready to answer my questions?

Mr. Donald: Yes, yes, fuck yes...god yes, yes, yes, yes.

George: Good to see that it worked. Now what do you remember about your last day?

Mr. Donald: I am not sure. I remember waking up. I had to go to the unemployment office, they didn't

---

want to give me my money. Something about never having worked.

George: You have never had a job, why should they pay you unemployment?

Mr. Donald: Cause it's the government, that's what they do. Anyway, I am a professional protestor.

George: You are a professional protestor? I bet your parents were proud.

Mr. Donald: I don't really know. My mom was upset because my dad was talking about kicking me out again. I don't know why. It's not like they use the basement for anything.

George: You lived in your parent's basement?

Mr. Donald: Yeah, I mean I am only twenty-four.

George: Yes, you are twenty-four. You went to the unemployment office?

Mr. Donald: Nah man, I didn't make it. I stopped over at my bro Tommy's house, his parents were out of town, so no one to hassle us.

George: You went to your ...ah "Bros" Tommy's house because his parents were out of town. How old was your friend?

Mr. Donald: He was like thirty. Anyway, he was all pissed about you demons abusing damned souls. It was all over Social Media… It was the happening thing.

George: The happening thing was demons abusing damned souls?

Mr. Donald: Yeah, everyone was talking about it trying to figure out how to protest it. I mean that is what we do.

George: What is it you do?

Mr. Donald: Protest. I have been to all kinds of protests. Someone has to protest for the oppressed.

George: Do you see yourself as a hero?

Mr. Donald: Kind of, I guess.

George: Go on about your day.

Mr. Donald: Me and Tommy smoked a little and kept reading all about how badly the damned were treated. Tommy was really into it. He kept trying to find out where the protest was and how we could get there. But no one online was coming up with anything.

George: What did you decide to do?

Mr. Donald: Tommy wanted to talk to a human rights group he knew of. They were a little wilder than what I normally did. But Tommy said they might have a good idea.

George: What do you mean wilder?

Mr. Donald: The group kind of liked to try and get into fights and stuff. Anything to get on the news.

George: Did they have an idea?

Mr. Donald: Not when we got there, they were all on their phones looking for an idea. But no one had any luck yet. I decided to smoke another joint, Tommy and one of the girls decided to help me with it.

George: You, Tommy and a girl who you didn't know were smoking marijuana, waiting for the group to come up with an idea?

Mr. Donald: Yeah, pretty much. We were only about halfway through when one of the guys came and got us. The group had an idea. They wanted to protest in Hell, that was where the problem was. What good was a protest if it wasn't where the issue was actually happening. Sure did make sense to me.

George: I am sure it made sense to you. How did they propose to get to Hell?

Mr. Donald: By the time we got back inside they had already figured it out. Suicide, one of the girls used to go to church a lot and said suicide was a sure way to go to Hell. It was simple we all commit suicide at the same time. We all go to Hell together. We all protest together, and we change things. It was a great plan.

George: It was a plan. Did anyone object?

Mr. Donald: A few did, but there are always a few to object.

George: How did you decide to do it?

Mr. Donald: We were gonna drink the Kool-Aid.

George: Can you explain that?

Mr. Donald: Well I think I can, so you know the saying "drink the Kool-Aid." It comes from a bunch of people that were so determined to follow an idea they actually drank poisoned Kool-Aid.

George: I don't think you understood what that was all about. There were nine hundred and eighteen people in Jonestown, Guyana drank cyanide laced Flavor Aid, and died.

Mr. Donald: Yeah that's the story, but we didn't have any cyanide. They did have a whole bunch of oxycodone. The group said it was just as good.

George: Were you worried at this point?

Mr. Donald: Hell no, I was gonna do what was right.

George: You were gonna do what you thought was right even if it killed you?

Mr. Donald: Man, it's never as bad as they say. Everyone said when I went to jail it was gonna be for years. I got out in six months. It's all exaggerated.

George: Continue with your memories.

Document 20 Interview: I234567-8760894

Mr. Donald: We were trying to decide when we wanted to do this. Several people were talking about leaving, but the rest of the group kept them there.

George: Some of the group didn't want to do it?

Mr. Donald: Like I said, there are always some that don't want to do anything. That is when a guy named Lucas made everyone lock the doors.

George: Is Lucas the leader?

Mr. Donald: There was no leader, Lucas just made things happen.

George: How did Lucas do that?

Mr. Donald: He just told people what to do.

George: Lucas started telling people what to do like what?

Mr. Donald: Like lock the doors, get the Kool-Aid. Give out the Oxycodone.

George: Did you get your Kool-Aid and Oxycodone?

Mr. Donald: Did I, six people give me extra pills they had. Said they wanted to share the experience. So nice, those people are so nice.

George: They sure seem really nice. What happened next?

Mr. Donald: We all got in a circle, there were like thirty or forty of us.

(George reviews a paper.)

George: Sixteen to be exact.

Mr. Donald: I thought there was more. Oh well, so Lucas is up there talking about how great this protest is gonna be. He tells us we are to take all the Oxycodone, and make sure and drink all the Kool-Aid. I asked, "are we gonna do it all together?" Lucas looked at me and said, "no one at a time. You are first."

George: Did you go first?

Mr. Donald: Sure did…

(Mr. Donald looks around the room, with a lost look on his face)

Mr. Donald: Sir, can I ask a question?

George: Go ahead and ask.

Mr. Donald: Where is the rest of the group?

George: You are the only one that actually took the pills or drank the Kool-Aid. Lucas had laced the Kool-Aid with rat poison. After you took the seven pills of Oxycodone, and drank all the Kool-Aid, your body went into some kind of shock. Watching you foam at the mouth and flop on the floor scared the rest of the group and they did not commit suicide.

Mr. Donald: Oh.

Afternote:

Mr. Donald's parents were anything but upset about their son's suicide. After a very short grieving period, his mother decided to help parents who are struggling with their kids' launches from home. The first stop was Tommy's parent's house. She assisted them on kicking him out onto the street.

Damnation Recommendation:

Recommend Mr. Donald be put to work moving rocks from one side of Hell to the other. One at a time. He should wear blinders so he can only see the rocks. He should not be able to interact with anyone or anything else. Recommend damnation review in one-thousand years.

Future books

If you enjoyed this pile of shit, just wait there's more. That's right, more shit coming your way. In the form of Chuck's story. The demon who brought you these shitty documents now gets his own story. Read how he was punished, how he survived roaming the earth for thousands of years, and how he partied like it was 1999 through it all.

From the Author

      I set out to write something that would make me laugh. I hope there is at least one person out there that laughs at the idiots I created in this book. I relished figuring out ways for them to die, and hope whoever reads this enjoys reading about how they died.

      If you find some of the characters frustrating and eerily similar to someone you have dealt with in the past, good, much of the inspiration came from dealing with frustrating idiots in the past.

      This collection started as a joke I was making with my lovely wife, it expanded from there. I tried to convince her to write something using the concept. She said a flat no, but that I should write it, so I did. When you see on the news and someone dies from doing something stupid you have to wonder how they would explain it. I always wanted to hear the explanations of some of the actions. Why did they pick a fight with the golden glove boxer, or did they NOT know Orcas are also known as Killer Whales? I am sure we will never know these answers.

      I hope you enjoyed my writing, and I hope you laughed at something. If not my writing, something, laughing is always good.

M. Maker

Printed in Great Britain
by Amazon